NOT THIS TIME

JEN TYES

Time is the coin of your life. It is the only coin you have, and only you can determine how it will be spent. Be careful lest you let other people spend it for you.

~Carl Sandburg (1878 - 1967)

Prologue

My life changed on a Sunday. It was the same as it had always been, an afternoon at my parents' estate. Bill and Maryann George were part of an elite group of people. My mother, Maryann, was an heiress who inherited a fortune when both her parents passed fifteen years ago and my father was head of cardiology at Handley Medical, where I, Emma George, am doing my residency. For years, my parents have proclaimed Sunday brunch a requirement and I gave into them to keep them off my back. As long as the other six days were mine to do as I pleased, I didn't mind giving them my Sundays. As I sat there, half-listening to the Sunday brunch conversation, my mind wandered to other places. I thought about my patients, my townhouse, I even thought about getting a pet I'd name Sammy, knowing full well I don't have the time to take care of it. *Would Sammy be a cat or a dog? Ooh! Maybe a hamster! I could take care of a hamster.*

Nothing bored me more than a conversation with my parents about money and status. They acted like there was nothing more in the world to focus on. It was always the same conversation. Politics, how the middle class is ruining this and that in the world, how their biggest problem in life is which private jet they will take to one of their private islands. It sickened me. I grew up knowing I was privileged, but I never took advantage of that fact. I didn't shop like crazy, I drove a modest car, I didn't carry any of those ridiculously expensive handbags my mother is always trying to get me to buy, and I gave money away to people who had better use for it. Besides, the money I grew up with belonged to my parents, so when I graduated from high school, I wanted to pay my way through life. I made sure to secure my life by planning strategically. I just wish my father would stop trying to make decisions for me. I know I shouldn't complain, because this is the way he shows his love, but it feels too much like he wants to run my life. My father insisted that he buy me a townhouse. I agreed, but told him that I would choose which to buy, and I would pay my mortgage. He agreed to pay the down payment, and I have been living on my own since I was eighteen years old. If it wasn't for my scholarship to college, I would have never been able to afford it, but I needed to show my father that I was capable of taking care of myself. Even after years of being responsible, my father still hasn't let up in my life. I'm not sure he ever will.

A voice interrupted my thoughts, "Emma! Em, are you listening?" I lifted my head and looked at my father, who was sitting across the table. "Sorry Dad, what were you saying?" My dad just smiled, jerked his head to his left to hint for me to look to my right. I glanced at my mother, who sat next to my father and was creepily beaming at me. I turned to my right only to find my boyfriend, Greg, on one knee, holding up a ring box. Greg began attending Sunday brunch shortly after we became serious. I actually believe he looks forward to Sunday each week, just so that he could rub elbows with my father and get on his good side. Greg never had to try hard. His ambitions were aligned with my parents', and in their eyes, he was a perfect fit into the family, and a great addition to Sunday brunch.

He grabbed my hand, "Em..." I held my breath and started looking around for an escape. He started again. "Em, I've loved you for a long time and I think we belong together. In fact, I know we belong together. I want to make this official. So what do you say, will you marry me?" I started shaking, and sweating from all parts of my body. This was too much pressure. Why didn't anyone give me heads-up on this whole thing? It was evident that my parents were aware of the proposal. Crap! Why was this happening today? My parents were looking at me, urging me to respond. My dad was looking at me with a look of approval and my mom was nodding her head slightly, as if she was answering for me. I was not ready for this step but as I looked into the faces around the table, I got the feeling that no one cared if I was ready or not. I felt cornered, so I knew what I had to say. I put on the bravest face and steadied my voice, "Yes!" The tears started to flow down my cheeks. My mother jumped up, hugged me, and stole me away to talk about engagement parties, bridal showers, and color schemes. She thought my tears were tears of joy, but that is not at all what I felt. What had I just gotten myself into?

Chapter One

I ARRIVED DOWNTOWN WITH 30 MINUTES TO SPARE. THE radio station was starting their listener's choice segment and the Prince song "Kiss" began to fill the speakers. I sat in my car, trying to think of an excuse to leave and drive back home, instead. *Did I leave the lights on? Am I catching a cold? Sore throat? Maybe I left the stove on...* So many random thoughts floating around my head. The last thought stuck inside my mind, even when I know I rarely have time to cook. I dismissed those thoughts because nothing solid had come to mind. The only option left was to go in and greet the room full of people.

I let out a breath. Things were not supposed to be this way. I reached for the door handle and the light from the street lamp caught the diamonds from the ring on my left hand. The ring began to weigh down my finger. Tonight was the night that Greg and I were going to announce our engagement to our closest friends. I sighed. I hated the big gawky thing. Greg had made a big fuss about the ring, he said, "You have to wear the best, if you're with the best."

He was so cocky. He was a 29-year-old junior partner at one of the largest firms in the East. He felt like everything that he touched turned to gold, and that everything in his life had to represent greatness. I tolerated that attitude because he was one of the greatest and moral lawyers that I knew. He was cocky because he thought that speaking and acting this way was the only way to get people to see his importance. He was in corporate law. He didn't represent corporations that want to have their wrong-doings erased, he represented corporations that stood for something and were on the right side of the law. He knew the law, and he made sure it was the law that won his cases. I admired him, but something pulled at me, telling me that I should hold off the wedding. There were things about Greg that I didn't love, but I knew that I was the type of person who could make a horribly incompatible arranged marriage work. We were newly engaged, but Greg wanted us to get married this summer. It was February and I felt that a June wedding was too soon. I was in the middle of my residency and didn't want to add "Wife" to my title before I completed my training. There were so many variables between us. I was working through my trust issues and know that I needed to fix that before marrying anyone. Greg seemed sure that he was ready and I was trying to convince myself that I was ready, too.

I couldn't shake the continuous thoughts about my past relationships, where I went wrong them, and what I was doing differently, now, that made this right. My reveries took me back to lunch today. The day started like all my others. I went to work like normal but, of all days, I decided to go to my favorite park for lunch since it was a fairly mild winter day. The park was just across the way from the hospital, so I took my homemade sandwich with my coat and scarf and sat on a bench in the gazebo. It was cold but because I was working a double, I needed the fresh air to keep me awake. As I was sitting there, eating my tuna sandwich and daydreaming, a bout of laughter brought me back to the present. I turned my head to see where it came from, when I spotted Jimmy and some woman. Our eyes met and I turned my head, hoping that he wouldn't notice me and come over. Jimmy. Jimmy was this guy that I dated my freshman year in college. He had rockstar hair that smelled heavenly and a pair of blue eyes you could stare into forever. The only problem I found with him was his rockstar reputation. I was in love with him, and I guess you can say the feeling was not mutual. I used to worship him and do whatever he wanted me to do. All I wanted from him was love, and he was too busy giving his "love" away to other women. I never understood how he could treat me like that, when all I did was give my heart to him. I guess some people are meant to love, while others are meant to take love and not reciprocate.

My worst fear came to pass when I heard my name from behind, "Emma! Emma! Is that you?" I turned to meet the voice. "Oh, it IS you!" I managed a small smile, hoping that I didn't have tuna in my teeth. "Hey, Jimmy, how's it going?" I stood up to greet him as he grabbed me into a hug. The woman he was with just stood there and glared at me. I couldn't do anything but give her a tentative smile. My guess was that she was the new flavor of the month. Jimmy could never stay long enough to get to know someone. I felt a little sorry for her.

"So Emma, How are you doing? Last I heard, you became a doctor... I can see that rumor was true." He gave me the once over, noticing my scrubs. I stepped back, putting two arm-lengths between us. "Oh yeah, I'm doing my residency at Handley Medical. I'm going into Pediatrics." He just beamed at me, making me a little uncomfortable with the attention. "I just can't believe I am seeing you right now." I looked behind him at the woman, who was obviously upset by his actions. I felt her pain, because I had been where she is. Jimmy had the attention span of a two-year-old. He had a way of forgetting you were there if something better came along. She loudly cleared her throat, that caused Jimmy to blink and break the enchantment. "Oh, I'm sorry. Where are my manners?" He laughed nervously, turned to the woman, and I couldn't help but think, *What manners?* "This is Kerry."

I held out my hand. She stepped forward, grabbing my hand with force. "His wife. I've heard so much about you," she said, with a hint of venom. She had a smirk on her face which caused me to blushed slightly. Jimmy had a wife! Jimmy was married. What universe am I living in where Jimmy found someone to spend the rest of his life with, and I am still questioning the length of time between engagement and marriage I am willing to give to Greg. "Nice to meet you, Kerry. I wish I could say the same, but I haven't spoken to Jimmy since undergrad. I see, now, that a lot has changed since we knew each other." I needed to give her some comfort, let her know that he was not in communication with me, and was different from what I remembered. I'm sure she knows about his past and his wandering ways. She was relieved at this revelation, but continued to glare. Jimmy stepped in to cut the tension. "Ahh, the good ol' days. Well, Kerry and I have been married for a while now, and we have two little ones at home."

A pang of jealousy hit me. It wasn't that I wanted to be with Jimmy. It was that he finally settled down and now has a family. I'm not sure what he does for a living, but from the looks of them, they aren't doing half bad. He has everything that I want, and it makes me jealous. I just wonder what would have been, if I had stuck with him after all that he put me through. Would I be in Kerry's shoes, and have two babies calling me mama? This was a turn of events. Curiosity is slicing through me, thinking about what could have been. Breaking my thoughts and plastering on a smile, I find my voice to speak, "That's great! Congrats! You must be very happy." Jimmy wasted no time responding, "Thanks, thanks.

What about you? Married, kids?" Sadness shadows me and I hoped that it wasn't showing on my face. I love kids, and want them so bad, but Greg isn't ready for that. He wants to wait until his name is on the building of his firm. I tried my best to look and sound happy, "No children, but I am engaged. Greg Turner, he's a junior partner over at TTC Attorney at Law. An emotion flashed over Jimmy's face, but was gone before I could identify it.

"Ahh, a big shot. Well, congrats to you."

I smiled. An awkward silence followed so I looked down at the ground until Jimmy broke it. "Well, it was nice seeing you, Em. Good luck with... everything." I smiled and waved as they walked away. "Thanks. And it was nice to meet you Kerry."

I sighed again as the memory faded. It was a very bizarre lunch hour, and only kept me thinking about my past boyfriends all afternoon. I began to wonder about all of them. What they were doing, where they worked, if they were married, with kids. After wondering about their current lives, I wondered about what could have been. All this reminiscing caused me to sigh. Noticing that I had yet to leave the car, I grabbed the handle and pulled to open the door. A gust of wind caught my face before I covered it up with my scarf. It is supposed to be one of the happiest moments in my life, and I cannot bring myself to be overly joyed.

I began walking toward the bar. It was almost like a typical Friday for us. Greg, a few of his co-workers, my best friend, Lyn, and I, when I was not on call, would meet at Max's for happy hour and sometimes stay for dinner. After Greg proposed at last Sunday's bunch, he decided that we should surprise our friends with the news at Friday's happy hour. So, here I am, walking to the bar about to announce my future. I stopped in front of the bar's first window. I could see the group in there, having drinks and laughing at jokes Greg was telling. I watched the scene from outside. I watched as Greg put his arm around Lyn's neck, as if it was the most natural action to take with your fiancé's best friend. Lyn didn't move. She, too, acted as if it was a natural thing to do.

Lyn was beautiful and very exotic looking. She had long, straight black hair, grey eyes, and dimples in each cheek. She was tall, with the body of a model. I never understood why she never pursued modeling. She would have been really good at it, she loved being the center of attention and in front of a camera. I stood there holding my breath. When my chest began to hurt, I let out a long breath and turned to walk away. I collided with an elderly gentleman. "Oh, excuse me, sir. My mistake." The man just smiled at me, "Oh, not a problem, miss. Say, are you all right? You look like you saw a ghost and tried to make a run for it." I couldn't help but laugh. I laughed at what this man said, laughed at myself, and laughed at the situation. "You know, you can't run from ghosts. You have to face them head on and deal with it. If not, they will just follow you around forever." I turned back to the scene in the bar. Nothing had changed. Everyone knew I was punctual, so they didn't expect me for another 20 minutes. The elderly man's voice close to my ear interrupted my thoughts, "You look like you could use a seat. If you like, I can sit with you for a while, until you get your bearings back." I looked at him, thankful to have some kindness at this moment. "Sure, I'd like that."

Chapter Two

He led me to a coffee shop a few doors down. Funny how I've been coming to Max's for years, and have never been to this coffee shop before. "Would you like a cup of coffee?" I wasn't a big coffee drinker but the smell of the coffee shop reminded me of a place of comfort. I gave him a weak smile, "Tea, please." He led me to a table, then walked away to order, leaving me alone to ponder. I was so lost in my thoughts. I didn't know what I should do. My mother would say to marry him, because he was a good man and a man of substance. Of course, she would say that. A man of "substance" is a man who can provide financially. She married my father because he was a man of substance. She's benefitted very well from his substance. There's no going to her for advice. I don't really have any friends to talk to. I lost touch with many of them when Greg and I got together and Lyn doesn't get personal with me much, anymore. As the picture becomes more clear, I'm sure it's because she and Greg have a thing going. What is wrong with me? I am so stupid! Why did I allow Greg to separate me from my friends? I am more alone than I have ever been. At least growing up as the only child, I had my nanny, even though I'd always wished I had siblings to play with. I knew if I had a sister, we'd be close and she would help me with this decision. I would have an ally supporting me and my dreams, instead of trying to force me into a mold. But instead, I have to figure life out on my own.

Breathing a sigh, I took in my surroundings. We sat down at a table, close enough to the window to see out but not close enough to be seen. This man was my savior and I didn't even know his name. Just as the thought passed, the elderly gentleman came around, placing the cup of tea in front of me. "There you are, miss." I grabbed the mug, placing my hands around it, taking in the warmth. This place was wonderful! I felt at home with the low lighting, comfy seats, nice jazz music, and real mugs to drink my tea out of. I felt myself relaxing a little. "Sir, you've been too kind. I don't even know your name. I'm Emma. Emma George."

He took his seat, "It's an honor to meet you, Ms. George. They call me Harold King. You can call me Harry." I smiled, then took a sip of tea. I guess I got lost in thought again because I snapped back into reality when Harry called to me, "Emma? Are you okay? What's eating at you?" I sighed, then rolled my eyes, trying to prevent the tears that were already forming in my eyes from falling. "Back at the bar, you saw me staring at the man that had his arm around that woman?" Harry nodded. "Well, that was my fiancé and my best friend, Lyn." I gave Harry a moment to catch on. When he did, his eyes widened, then filled with sorrow and he grabbed my hands, giving them a squeeze.

I looked down at my tea and began speaking, "You know, we have been dating for almost four years now... and Lyn... she's been my friend since high school. He thinks I don't know what's going on. And she forgets that I've known her for almost forever. I'm not completely oblivious to the world around me. I only agreed to marry him because my parents wanted me to. I love him... but I don't think I'm in love with him. I just wish I had the guts to speak up for myself." I took a sip of tea. I looked up to find Harry looking at me with bewilderment. My face heated up with embarrassment. I don't even know this man and I feel more comfortable around him than anyone in my life. I shouldn't be laying my heavy drama on a complete stranger, but yet here I am. Harry doesn't deserve any amount of my crazy so I feel the need to apologize. "Harry, I am so sorry. I don't even know you and here I am airing out my dirty laundry," I exhale deeply and loudly. "It's just... I have no one to speak to. I allow Greg to make decisions for me and when he's not making decisions, my parents are. I used to talk to Lyn about my issues, but once Greg got whiff of it, he demanded that I stop sharing so much about our life. I stopped, of course. That's what good Stepford wives are supposed to do. I don't really have a mind of my own... I want to work for Doctors

Without Borders, or like a free clinic in the inner city, but he feels that I'm needed here so he worked with my father to get me the residency position at the prestigious Handley hospital, in the award-winning Pediatrics department." I rolled my eyes. "I don't even know who I am."

I put my head on the table and covered it with my arms and blew out a breath. The tears began to flow freely now. It was a revelation that I was not ready to face. Who am I? For the last few years, I have been an extension of Greg. Before that, I was an extension of whoever I was with, and before that, I was an extension of my parents. I didn't have a unique identity. I am a poor excuse for a person. I felt Harry's hand pat my head. I reluctantly raised my head and met Harry's concerned face. He handed me a napkin. I must have been a fright with my makeup smearing and mascara running, but it didn't stop me from continuing. "I ran into an ex today. He cheated on me throughout our whole relationship and when I finally had enough, I left him and went about my life." I shrugged my shoulders and tilted my head. "I met his wife today." I had to laugh at the irony. I wasn't enough, so he cheated and now he was married, probably faithful, with kids. "They seemed very happy together and they have kids! I want kids!" I sank back into silence. "Did you wish you were her?"

I looked up at Harry after he spoke. Did I wish I were Kerry? It was a good question, I hadn't even thought about it fully yet. "Yes... well, not really." I sat back and chewed on my fingernail, thinking of how to best clarify my answer. "It's just that I wish I had the kind of easy-going relationship with someone who shared the same values and timeline as me. I want to start a family, and not when I'm 35. I want a career in something I love. I want to laugh in the park at lunchtime." I felt like I had revealed too much. I looked pleadingly into Harry's eyes, "Is that too much to ask for?" It was a rhetorical question, but part of me wanted Harry to provide me with an answer that would put me at ease.

He gave me a small smile before grabbing my hands. "What is it that you really want?" Now that was the million-dollar question. How was I supposed to answer this without rattling on and on about the failed relationships in my life, and why all of them failed? After seeing Jimmy, I just had so many what-ifs floating around my head. I thought about my past, and how I handled myself and what I could have done differently. If only I could travel in a time machine and stop myself from making stupid mistakes, or missing an opportunity. So much of my life could be changed if I could just go back in time with the knowledge that I had. Hindsight is 20/20, and I wish I could share some of this knowledge with my younger self. Harry looked at me with expectant eyes. I couldn't wrap my brain around it all, but I'd try my best. "Well, if I could, I would love to revisit my failed relationships and see what went wrong. I guess I would first like to visit the guy in the present, to see how he turned out. But taking a peek at the past would help me to understand where I came from, and how I got to this juncture in my life."

I sighed, "I dunno. I guess I am really bothered by so

many what-ifs after seeing my ex, Jimmy, today, that I wonder if I let a great guy go before I realized his potential for me." I sighed again, "Silly, huh?" I chuckled nervously. Harry was going to think I was a nut job. He was going to get up and walk out the door, and not even look back. We stared at each other for a passing moment when all of a sudden Harry began to laugh out loud. "My dear, Emma. This is not as silly as you think." I raised an eyebrow at him. Now, I'm not too sure I'm the only crazy one at the table. "What do you mean, Harry? That is impossible to do. I can only dream." He stopped laughing and gave me a serious look. "You can and you will... if you want to." I raised my eyebrow again, "Huh?" Harry leaned in close to whisper, "What if I told you that you can see your exes as they are in the present, revisit your past relationships, and see a possible outcome considering you had stayed in the relationships?" I leaned in close to whisper, "What, are you going to sit here and tell me that you are the ghost of boyfriends past and you are here to show me all the wrong I've done in past, present, and future relationships, so that I can make things right with my one true love?" I let out a tiny giggle. "I've seen that movie. Matthew McConaughey was pretty hot in that one."

Harry looked at me soberly. "Come on, Harry. Do you really believe that I can do that? I'm a doctor in training, not a miracle worker... Although some people may think that I am because I am a doctor." I screwed up my face as I analyzed my last statement. Harry straightened up in his chair, "Well, I was only trying to help you. Since you don't really need my help, I will leave you to your evening." He began to stand, to grab his coat. I reached out and grabbed his arm, "Wait, Harry. Please sit." I pleaded with my eyes. He hesitated, but finally sat down. "I was not trying to make fun... well too much fun. It's just that I don't understand what you mean. Maybe if you show me." He brought his index finger and thumb up and stroked his chin. "Well, this is unorthodox but I think it should be fine. Once you see what I have to show you, you will want to see the rest." I was instantly intrigued.

Chapter Three

I FELT LIKE I SHOULD BE NERVOUS, BUT FOR SOME reason, I wasn't nervous at all. I was ready to see what Harry had to show me. I was looking for an answer anywhere I could, and Harry may be my answer, even if I didn't believe that he was going to show me anything.

"Okay, Emma. You must have an open mind. You said you ran into Jimmy today. I want you to focus on him." I closed my eyes and saw his face. There he was, Jimmy in all his glory. Those blue eyes melting my heart. Oh, how I wish he was faithful when we were dating. I could scarcely hear Harry speaking to me, because I was so lost in Jimmy's eyes. I paused as I felt off-balance. I opened my eyes and noticed something terribly different. The background, that was a blur, began to come into focus. I blinked repeatedly to clear the fog and take in my surroundings. I was no longer in the coffee shop, but back at college, standing in Jimmy's dorm room. It was like I was watching a movie. I was there, but not really there, in the room. Deep down inside me, I instinctively knew what day it was. It was the first and last time I had found Jimmy with another girl. I knew that he had been flirting with other girls, but never had any proof other than my friends and classmates telling me. I had always been a "seeing is believing" kind of person so, although somewhere in the back of my mind I knew that Jimmy was unfaithful, I couldn't bring myself to react to it until I saw it.

The scene played out in front of me, stringing me along as a passive participant. I was in my younger body, yet was still able to look around and feel like I was not actually part of whatever this was I was experiencing. Jimmy's roommate had let me in, telling me that he thought Jimmy had come into the suite ten minutes ago and was in his room. I remember this day like it was yesterday, and recall that I didn't think anything of my actions. I just walked into his room, like I always do, and was confronted with the scene in front of me.

It was my friend Sasha who was straddling him on his bed. I stood there frozen, unable to speak. Jimmy was laying down on the bed, running his hands all over Sasha's body and he began to assist her in taking off her shirt. With her shirt off, Jimmy rose up to meet her lips, but saw me, instead. He un-ceremoniously pushed Sasha off his lap and onto the bed. As Jimmy got up and started putting on his clothes, he said, "This is not what it looks like." I couldn't find anything to say, but I felt the warm tears flowing down my cheeks. Jimmy cautiously approached me, "She doesn't mean anything to me." I heard a very loud huff in disagreement come from behind him. He turned around, I guess to give her a look to silence her, then turned back to me. "Emma, I don't love her. I just... God, Emma." He brought his hands to his head and groaned in anger, "I needed some release. She's been helping me deal with it." He came up to me and grabbed my hands, "I love you so much and want to be with you... and I know that you are waiting to have sex... I just can't wait. I'm a man with needs." Although it was like a movie for me this time around, I still felt the pain from his admission. I wanted to ask him why and wanted to express my anger verbally, but something was preventing me and all I could do was cry. The worst pain was yet to come. I was about to watch myself walk out of the room, out of Jimmy's life, and cry myself to sleep for a month. I avoided him for the rest of the semester, until he was no longer interested in me. Then, when he no longer tried to seek me out, I cried even harder and slipped into a depression.

I tried to brace myself for that pain, but it never came. Jimmy grabbed my hands. As I witnessed the scene, I saw myself, instead of slipping my hands out of Jimmy's hands and turning to walk away, I slipped my hands out and stood there. It was all the forgiveness Jimmy needed. He turned and told Sasha to get out and never return. He even added, "And you call yourself a friend," with distaste. I did nothing as Sasha angrily put her shirt back on and stomped out of the room, yelling, "Fuck you, asshole!" I felt satisfaction in him telling her to leave. But this was not how it happened in my memories. As the scene progressed, I was intrigued to see how I finished it off. In my mind, I tried so many times to see how things could have been done differently and finally, here it is! Jimmy took my hand and led me to the bed. I hesitated, so he led me to the desk chair, instead. He got down on the floor, still embracing my hands. Taking two deep breaths, he spoke, "Em, I see now how I have been hurting you. You're crying and haven't said two words to me... it's killing me. You didn't walk out, so I take it as a sign that you want to work it out." I felt stupid at that moment, but did nothing to change that feeling. I could have said anything yet, instead, I sat there silently.

Jimmy took the silence as agreement and continued, "I know you don't trust me. But believe me when I say that I will make it up to you. I meant it, when I said I loved you." With trust in my heart, I muttered my first words all afternoon, "I love you, too." At that moment, all I wanted was Jimmy, and my heart broke a little knowing that when this dream was over, reality would kick in and I'd be back at square one of my problem. The room began to blur and I lost all emotions attached to the events that just occurred.

The next thing I knew, my life was flashing before my eyes and I was back in the coffee shop, where Harry is looking at me, waiting.

Chapter Four

I was smiling and crying tears of joy. I couldn't believe what I just saw. *Was it real? If it was real, how was it real?* I looked to see that Harry was still waiting. "So, what did you think?" *What did I think? Did my imagination run away from me?* I had so many questions, but I guessed I could begin by telling Harry what I thought. "Well, ... I thought it was very interesting. I mean, I don't really understand what happened because I thought I was just reliving my past. When the scene changed, it was like I was finally seeing what I've been trying to imagine since Jimmy and I broke up. How did you do that?" Harry sat back with a smug smile on his face. "It's called AUV travel." I looked at him, puzzled. "What is 'Off' travel?" I asked. He added laughter to his smile. "It's AUV travel, not 'off'," he said, drawing out each letter sound. "AUV is an acronym for Alternate Universe View. It might be easier to think of it like time traveling. You get to see the past, as well as a version of the past and future, if certain actions are changed." I let the words sink in. "I just time traveled, and what I saw would have been my present, if I'd just forgiven him?"

Shaking his head, "Well, it's a little more complicated than that. See, what you saw was ONE outcome of the past, present, and future. Say, do you mind telling me what you saw?" I thought back to what I had seen. "It felt like I lived another lifetime. I don't remember it all, like when I wake up from a dream, but basically, I forgave Jimmy, he took the rest of college proving his loyalty to me. We got married right after undergrad. My parents didn't approve of him, so I was cut off. He got a job and supported me through med school, except I found out I was pregnant during the first semester of my second year, so I dropped out to become a stay-at-home mom. If this was my life, I'd have two children right now, and one on the way."

Harry sat back to ponder what was spoken. "Emma, how do you feel about that outcome?" It was a lot to take in. AUV traveling, seeing the life I could have had, but actually belongs to some other me. Technically, it's a life that I'm living, but sort of living it on some other dimension. It was all confusing, but I knew for sure that I wanted to know more. I took a deep breath and revisited what I saw. "It made me feel like an individual. There was no one making decisions for my life, but me. Although that life is not the life I have in mind for myself, I think that it was an okay start to what you have to show me. Is there more? Will you let me see all my past relationships, and how things could have been?" I could barely contain my excitement. Harry just smiled at me before speaking, "If you would like to see some other outcomes to past relationships, I can do that for you. What you do with the knowledge is up to you." My smile reached ear to ear, "Well, sign me up!" Harry motioned for me to stand up. "We can't do it here. My place of business isn't far. Let's go." I gathered my coat and scarf. We walked out the door and turned right, further and further away from Max's. Although I was aware of the fact that I was blowing off my fiancé and friends on the night we were to announce our engagement, I felt like I had more important things to attend to.

On the next block, Harry stopped in front of a small shop. Though the shop was small, there was a set of glass doors and a small display window that housed an array of clocks with signs about tradition. "You own a watch and clock store?" I looked at him in disbelief. It was just weird that he was talking about time travel and he owns a shop that deals with time. "I have to make a living like everyone else." We both laughed as he opened the door. I walked in and saw glass cases filled with all types of watches to match all types of personalities. There were clocks on top of the cases and along the walls. The room was filled with an array of ticking sounds, like a symphony of time. Harry locked the front doors and ushered me to the back. "I don't want people thinking that I'm open. Please, come to the back and get more comfortable." He showed me to a room that looked like a sitting room. There was a floral couch, two leather armchairs, and a glass table in the middle. It was very cozy. I took my coat and scarf off and sat on the couch. Instantly, I felt at home. "This is nice, Harry." He nodded thanks as he left the room. He came back with a blanket, a pillow, and a box of tissues. "This is going to be trying for you. You may see things that you wish you hadn't, and you may feel things that may bring pain or suffering." I arched my eyebrow at him, "What are you saying?" He took a deep breath and let it out. "I'm saying that I can't control which outcome you see. As I said, there is an outcome for every decision you have made. I never know which one you will experience and some outcomes are not always as positive, like the one you've seen."

My chest constricted and my heart began to beat fast. "Does this mean my death? What if I died in another life? Would I feel my death?" I started hyperventilating. "Can I be dead somewhere in the universe and not know it?" Harry put his hands on my shoulders, to try to calm me. "Dear Emma. You would never experience the death of an alternate you. That I am sure of. I just don't want you to expect the outcomes to all be roses and ponies. There is good and bad in the universe, and their balance must be maintained. There wouldn't be a balance if every decision you made led you to a positive or agreeable future. I just wanted to give you a warning." I sighed in relief. It made perfect sense. This is life, and life isn't always great. Taking a deep breath I said, "Okay, I'm ready." He told me to lie down on the couch and relax. "We will do two from your past and also your present relationship." I sat up in shock, "Why Greg?" Harry smiled at me, then patted my arm. "I'm throwing Greg in as a bonus." Satisfied with his response, I laid back down and Harry continued. "Right now, I need the names of two ex-boyfriends. I want you to speak their names out loud and picture them in your mind. Speak slowly and clearly. You understand?" I nodded, took a deep breath, and pictured my high school sweetheart.

He was perfect. He had dirty blond hair and beautiful tanned skin. The last time I saw him, he had the body of a God, muscles on muscles and extremely yummy. We were both home from first-semester break and saw each other at the grocery store. We spoke briefly and said we would get together, but never did. I think he may have met someone and didn't want to make things weird. After high school graduation, we only broke up because he was going to college across the country, I was staying local and neither one of us believed in long distance relationships. He was a sweet guy, with a southern upbringing. He believed in worshipping his woman and I loved him for being such a gentleman. I can't wait to see what life would have been with him. As I thought about him, I spoke his name, "Alex, Alexander Brown."

I took a breath and thought about the next troubling relationship. The guy I seriously dated after Jimmy. I was so scared of being cheated on that I only went on a few dates with guys before just calling the whole thing off. My next serious relationship after Jimmy was with a guy I knew since day one of college. I never thought about dating him until he took me out for pizza one night and we kissed. I still remember his full lips. He was the embodiment of tall, dark, and handsome. He was a little over six feet tall, with caramel skin and chocolate brown eyes. He had dimples on both cheeks that showed whenever he was laughing, and he was always laughing. I really cared about him. He knew how to make me laugh, even on my darkest days. He was there for me when Jimmy cheated. He was loyal to my heart but I could never shake the feeling of dread whenever we weren't together. In the back of my mind, I always worried about being cheated on. I knew he was loyal, but in the end, I just couldn't handle the stress of worrying. We broke up at the end of undergrad, yet remained distant friends until we eventually lost touch. As I thought about him, I spoke his name, "Bruce Johnson." The air around me began to change. Harry instructed me to close my eyes. "Now, Emma, I want you to continue focusing on Bruce. We will visit him first. With each trip, it will get easier and you will find that you may be able to control your surroundings, as well. Stay focused and keep an open mind." I closed my eyes and, instantly, I was no longer in Harry's cozy sitting room.

Chapter Five

BRUCE

I opened my eyes to see that Harry and his cozy room had, indeed, disappeared. I looked around and found that I was in the living room of an apartment. It was a nice apartment, despite the mounds of boxes stacked around the room. There were a few pictures that were still out. I walked up and grabbed the closest one. It was one of Bruce and a woman I have never met. She was someone that I could see with Bruce. She was young, with gentle, knowing green eyes and long brunette hair. The woman looked like she could possibly be pregnant. She had a small frame, but the look of someone who had eaten too much. Then a thought hit me. Bruce looked a little older, so this must be his present. I tried to remember the instructions that Harry had given me, but was coming up short, so I guessed I'd just go with the flow.

I tried to remember as much as I could about what Bruce and I had discussed the last time we spoke. It had to have been years, but I do know he was going to medical school after undergrad. I don't remember where he went, but I know he was doing well. I think he wanted to do his residency in general surgery. If that was still true, he should be in his third year, like me. I looked around to see if I could find some evidence. After searching for a few minutes, I found Bruce's old school bag. "He still has this old thing!?" I said, laughing to myself. I covered my mouth to silence myself, you never know. I bent down to the bag. I felt awful for snooping, but luckily, I didn't have to go into his bag. His ID badge was clipped to the outside and read *Third Year resident at Houston Medical*. I was sitting in what looked like Bruce's apartment, that he possibly shared with this mystery pregnant woman. She had a ring on her finger, so I knew they were engaged, but that's all I knew.

A bout of laughter broke me out of my thoughts and echoed down the hall. "Bruce stop it! You're going to make me pee my pants." The laughter continued, so I followed it. As I got closer, it was evident that the couple was moving. "Bruce, if you don't stop making me laugh, we are going to have this baby in this old apartment, instead of our home. Is that what you want?" I heard Bruce laugh and I panicked. It had been so long since I'd heard his laugh. It just made me remember how much I missed it, how much I missed Bruce.

I found the room where the source of the laughter was occurring. I placed my back to the wall, next to the door frame. "No, baby. I don't want you giving birth here. Especially since I skipped that rotation at the hospital. I wouldn't know what to do!" She laughed. "It's late, honey. We have a very big day ahead of us and I still have to study for the bar. You know I have scheduled an hour a day to study. The test and the baby will be here before we know it!" There was movement in the room. "I know, I know. I'm just so happy. Everything's coming together." I could hear Bruce's smile in his words. He was truly happy. I should be ecstatic for him, but it just made me sad that I missed an opportunity because I couldn't see past Jimmy's mistakes. "Okay, sweetie. I will leave you to your studies. But know that I will be back in an hour to read to the baby." They kissed. "Okay, Reggie. I'll see you in an hour." It was cute that she used a pet name from his middle name, Reginald. I'd always thought that Reginald was too proper, and Bruce was too short for a traditional nickname, so I called him Brucey. Lame, I know. I heard footsteps approaching and I began to panic. What would he say if he saw me standing here, eavesdropping on such a private and intimate moment? I tried to calm my heart and elected to run and hide.

I BEGAN to run back down to where I had come from, only to see that the scene had changed. I was in my college apartment I rented during my senior year of undergrad. I stopped in mid-stride and took a look around. It felt weird to be back in my old apartment. It was a great apartment, where I had all the privacy and quiet that I wanted. "Emma, please tell me what's wrong... I beg you!" Oh, no! I remember this day all too well. It was the day I broke up with Bruce. Well, technically, the day Bruce and I broke up. I walked over to the living room, to where the voices were coming from. I stayed out of sight, just in case this was different from what I experienced with Jimmy. "Bruce, we just don't spend enough time together. You are working, studying, and just so focused on everything, more so than focused on me. I don't know what to think half the time. You know me, and how it's very difficult for me to trust people after you-know-who. I'm always worried that I'm not enough for you." I saw my head dip in shame.

"Honey bear, you know that I have always been on your side. I have done everything in my power to make sure you know that I love you. I'm so sorry that you feel like I don't give you enough attention. I have to work to pay for school, and I have to study to make sure I keep my grades up. Don't you understand that I am doing this all for you, for us and our future?" Silence. "Em, I know what Jimmy did to you was unspeakable, and he's a bastard for putting you through it, but you have to know that I am different. I would never do anything like that to hurt you. Please say you know that." Bruce was pleading with me and all I was doing was crying into my hands. He continued, "I'd do anything to make you happy, but I can't quit my job and I need to keep my study sessions going. I hope you understand why I need to do this." Here it comes. Bruce was so heartbroken and lost when I refused to speak that he just broke it off with me, telling me to come to find him when I was ready to talk.

I braced myself for the pain that would follow. "Okay, Emma. Have it your way." He began to walk past the other me, toward the door. Although I didn't want to watch, I couldn't tear my eyes away from the scene. I was ready for it. Bruce was going to turn around, have finals words, then leave out the door and never return. Bruce turned and, before he could start talking, the other me ran up to him, knocking him back into the door and kissed him passionately. The kiss lasted for almost two minutes and began to heat up. Her hands were trailing under his shirt. I remember what those abs felt like. His hands were caressing her breasts and attempting to take off her shirt. I was still a virgin at that time, so I knew I was a bit timid. Just as the thought crossed my mind, the kiss ended. "Brucey, I'm so sorry. I love you and I understand. I'm just so crazy about you and afraid of losing you." She spoke the truth. I let things end between Bruce and me because I was afraid of losing him, and I lost him anyway. "Baby, I was there and I know how it has affected you. I'm here and I will take care of you." They began to kiss again, but this time it was filled with a passion I had yet to experience at this age. The other me ended the kiss and took Bruce by the hand, leading him toward the bedroom. "Are you sure, Em?" She nodded and continued toward the bedroom. The room began to fade, but I was sure that she was not going to be a virgin after that night.

I FOUND myself in the living room of a beautiful modern home, somewhere in a suburb. I looked around to find that there wasn't a thing out of place. It was gorgeous enough to be on display, yet still livable. There was a fireplace in the center of the longest wall. It was adorned with picture frames so I moved closer to see what the pictures were of. As I got closer, I began to recognize some faces. I reached out and picked up the closest one. It was of Bruce, myself, and two beautiful young boys. The boys had the same caramel skin complexion as their father, but had my hazel eyes. I think they were twins because, though there were differences, they looked to be the same age. They all looked so happy. I felt a tear wet my cheek. This was yet again another life that could have been mine. It was obvious that Bruce was doing well for himself. I wondered what had come of me. Did I complete my school work and residency? I looked around for anything that would show me what I did, show me where we lived. I looked and looked and found nothing. I heard laughter from another room. I followed the voices and stood outside the door. "Dad, if you don't stop tickling me, I am going to tell Mom on you." The laughter continued. "I'll just tickle your brother then. What do you say about that?" More laughter, this time from the other child. "What is going on boys?" The other me entered from an adjoining room. "Nothing, Mom." Then Bruce chimed in, "We were just having a little fun, Em. Would you like to join us?" Bruce held his hand out.

The other me just looked at the stretched out hand. "No, thank you. I'll just be in the other room." Then I left. This was a little confusing. What happened to the lovable me, and why did I sound so depressed? "Mom's never any fun anymore since the accident. Will she ever be fun again?" An accident! What accident? "Boys, your mother loves you very much, but she loved Anna, too. She's still a little sad that Anna's not here with us anymore. She will be fun again, I promise." He gave each boy a kiss, "Good night." The boys said okay in agreement and Bruce walked toward the direction that the other me went.

I walked to the other doorway and peeked in to try to get a clue. The room was pink and filled with all types of girly things. It was a room for a little princess, and my best guess was that it was Anna's room. Bruce entered the room and walked toward where the other me was sitting on a twin size bed, holding a doll. He spoke in a hush tone. "Em, I understand that you are hurting right now, but your other children, right in the other room, need their mother. They don't think you love them now that Anna's gone." The other me spoke in the same tone, "Bruce, I do love them. I just don't understand why this had to happen to our little girl. She was only three." I took a deep breath, "How is it that two doctors, married to each other, can't see that their own child is sick? How did we not recognize the signs?" Coming to sit next to me, Bruce reached out and grabbed my hands. "She had cancer, Em. Sometimes you don't see the signs until it's already too late. She didn't suffer long, and that's the important part. We need to be thankful that we were blessed to have her in our lives for the time we had. I love you, and we will get through this, but you have to help me." She began to cry and I mimicked her tears. Bruce consoled her and they laid together in little Anna's bed. The room began to fade, but the tears continued to flow.

I WAS ONCE AGAIN on Harry's couch, in his cozy sitting room. I sat up and looked at Harry as he handed me the box of tissues. "Are you all right, Emma?" I nodded, not trusting my voice. "Take your time. Let me know when you are ready to see the next one." Harry left the room, and left me with my thoughts. It was much more confusing this time around. I watched a possible future with Bruce and didn't "live" it, like I did when I saw my life with Jimmy. Although that life was not exactly perfect, it was a great life to have and I was sad that I wasn't strong enough to voice my wants and needs when the opportunity was there. I just couldn't shake the thoughts that went back to Little Anna. I didn't see any pics of her but I saw an image of a little girl and she was as beautiful as the boys, but with my curly brown hair and her father's brown eyes. I guess in a way it was good that Bruce and I aren't together. Maybe Anna will be born to someone else and live a nice, long, fulfilled life. Harry came back into the room as I finished praying for Anna to have a long and healthy life.

"Are you ready for the next installment?" I nodded, then said, "But first can you tell me why this travel was different from the one with Jimmy?" Harry sat down, "How was it different?" I looked at him, a little puzzled. "Well, with Jimmy, I was in the scenario as a participant, and with Bruce, I was able to move around and see myself or the other me. It was confusing, I didn't know if I should refer to her as me or "other" me or her, because it really wasn't me. I was standing there watching like a creeper..." I blew out an exaggerated breath. Harry looked at me and smiled, "With AUV, it's all about how deep the connection is. I'm not saying that you had a deeper relationship with Jimmy, or you didn't love Bruce enough. Ah, what I mean to say is, every experience will be different. You were able to experience a different outcome with Jimmy, partially because you were very emotional after running into him today. Your interactions with Bruce were probably not as recent." I nodded in under-standing. "Are you ready now?" he asked, letting out the breath he was apparently holding, so I responded with, "As ready as I'll ever be." I laid back and took a few deep breaths. "Now close your eyes and think about Alexander Brown." I closed my eyes and again, the cozy room was like a distant memory.

Chapter Six

ALEX

Harry and his cozy sitting room is once again gone and I found myself somewhere else. It was a very rundown apartment, in what looked like a very bad part of whatever town I was in. This must be Alex's present, but I was puzzled to find it in shambles. He was an A+ student in high school, and he did rather well in college, majoring in finance. The last I heard, Alex was working for a fortune 500 company, making six figures. I just could not figure out what turn of events made his life look like this. I had tried to keep up with his life, but this was not the home of a successful businessman. I looked around the room. It wasn't a very large apartment. It was an open floor plan, with two doors to my left. One led to a bathroom, and what I presumed was the bedroom. To my right was a kitchen, I was standing in the living room area and behind the living room was a table. The table was littered with paper and clutter. I never knew Alex to be a messy person, but it would appear that I didn't know this Alex at all.

I walked over to the table, to maybe find something that would help me better understand the situation. There was so much clutter that I didn't know where to start. I tentatively put my hand out to touch the mess. Success! I sifted through the paper until I found something with Alex's name on it. It was a bank statement, but the balance was in the negatives. I grabbed the chair to steady myself on my feet, causing a piece of clothing to fall. I picked it up and noticed it was a uniform shirt from a grocery store, with Alex's name on it. I blinked to try to clear what I was seeing. I simply could not believe my eyes. Just as I was putting the shirt back onto the chair, I heard keys unlocking the front door. My heart started pounding as I tried to make myself invisible. I tried not to imagine what Alex could possibly look like. Instead, I tried to continue thinking on how I remembered him... dirty blond hair, muscles for days, and a tan that every man dreams about. When the door finally opened, a short blond woman walked in the door, dressed in a waitress uniform. She was cute enough, with her pixie haircut and vivid green eyes. She walked in, straight to the kitchen, looking as if she'd been awake for days. "Honey, I'll make dinner, then rub your feet. What do you want to eat?" As if on cue, Alex walked in. A flash of sadness crossed his face as he looked upon the room. He looked almost the same, except for the fact that he looked like he'd had a hard life. His grey eyes were almost void of life, he wore a few days' old scruff, and he looked a little flabby. He still looked like he had his charm, but it was locked away for a better day. I had tears in my eyes as I watched him walk in with his back slumped. He walked right into the living room, sat in a worn recliner, and turned on the television. "I'll eat whatever you cook, baby. You know me." I thought I heard her mumble something but I missed it because I was watching Alex so intently. While Alex reclined in his chair in front of the TV, the woman in the kitchen slaved away at a meal.

Once she was finished, she went over to Alex, took his boots off and rubbed his feet. He closed his eyes and relaxed a little more. The whole scene was nice, because it gave me relief that Alex at least found love. Alex opened his eyes and looked down at the girl with intense desire in his eyes. He grabbed her by her hair and brought her up to his face, into a very hard and passionate kiss. I was confused, initially, because she appeared to fight him but after a short moment, she relaxed into his kiss and gave into him with the same amount of passion and fire. The event was getting to be too much for me. There was so much passion in the room. Alex became forceful, causing her to scream out. I wasn't sure if it was passionately rough, or plain rough, but before I could see more and understand what was really happening, the scene began to fade.

I FOUND MYSELF AT MY PARENTS' house and it was

just as I had seen it after high school. My mother upgraded the decor every couple of years, so there was no confusing the time period. I was in my room. Looking at it now, it looks so pathetic and juvenile. I have pictures of friends on my walls and pictures of boy bands that I thought were dreamy. I even had a picture up from my sweet sixteen. It made me so happy to see it. It was of me and my best friend, Lyn, and the singer Rox Star. He was so cute and had a number one single on the charts. My father had surprised me at my party. I thought that Rox Star's song was being played by the DJ, but it was actually Rox Star coming up from behind the stage, singing to me. I never screamed so loud in my life. Stuck in memory lane, I didn't even realize that the younger me was in the room until my mom called for me. "Coming, Mom!" We both said in one voice, which was a very weird experience. She rolled off the bed and threw the Science magazine without looking, and it toppled onto a pile of biology books. Even when I tried to be cool and like all regular teenage girls, I was still a nerd looking at school books and science magazines.

I followed her out the door, where I saw my cap and gown hanging from atop the door. I think I was in the day where Alex and I broke up. My shoulders hunched over because I was not ready to view this. I followed myself downstairs anyway. Curiosity got the best of me, because I knew that the ending was not going to be the ending that I remembered. We reached the end of the stairs to meet Mom. "Alex is in the sitting room waiting for you." The younger me beamed. She ran to the sitting room, then wrapped her arms around Alex's neck, before kissing him with the fullest. Mom cleared her throat and the younger me let go of young Alex and led him to the couch, without giving Mom a single glance. "So tell me, why the impromptu visit? I didn't expect to see you until later today for dinner." Alex looked nervous. "I have something to tell you, Em." She grabbed his hands and waited for him to continue. He took a deep breath, "Remember a few months ago, when we were talking about my college choices, and what would happen if I didn't get into a school close to here?" The younger me nodded. "Well, I got into all the schools I applied for b..." She squealed, "That's great!!! We can be together like we planned."

Young Alex's face stayed grim. "Look, Em, there's bad news. I haven't told you the worst part. I haven't said anything to you yet, because I was hoping to work things out, but I have to go to Wortmouth University. It's the only school that is giving me enough money to attend. I'm so sorry, Em." Younger me began to cry. "Oh, Alex, that's three thousand miles away. Why didn't you tell me? This is horrible. Isn't there anything you can do?" He shook his head, "My grades weren't what my father wanted them to be, and because we had a deal when I started high school, he is not going back on it. He is only giving me a certain amount each year, and I can't find a way out of it." I remembered that deal he had with his father. Mr. Brown was a financial genius. He made his money off buying and selling real estate. He was very forceful in his discipline of his children and wife. Mr. Brown also kept a good scotch close by. I witnessed some of the abuse with my own eyes. He was very strict and kept his word, no matter what. The deal was to graduate with a B+ or higher, and he would pay whatever educational expenses for college. Anything under a B+ would significantly lower the financial assistance. I thought Alex graduated with a B average and it just wasn't good enough for his father, so he set out after high school to prove his father wrong, and I thought that was what he had done.

The younger me stopped crying for a moment. "So I guess this is it. We have the summer, and then we're done?" Okay, this was it, the last nail to hit the coffin. "I'm so sorry, babe. I wish there was something I could do." That's different. He was supposed to say: *No. I think that it would be best not to drag things out.* We sat there for a few breaths, before the young me's eyes lit up. "You know what? Maybe we can work together and either get me into a school near you, or you into a school near me. What do you say? I'm sure my dad would help us." Young Alex smiled and hugged the younger me tighter. "Em, I don't want any handouts. I want to do this on my own. I need to be strong for us. If your father helps, it won't be just given to me. I will work for everything." There was determination in his voice, and I smiled at the scene as it began to fade.

I FOUND myself in a dark room of an unknown apartment.

There was no movement in the room, but I could hear the retreat of a pair of shoes and then the slam of a door. Something did not feel right. Slowly, a quiet sob could be heard from one corner of the room. I did not like the sound of those sobs. The situation just wasn't sitting right with me. First, the slamming of the door, and then the crying in a dark room. I didn't think that this was the happy ending I was hoping for. There was movement from the sobbing corner. There was some stumbling and wall groping. Finally, there was a silhouette in an adjoining room I guessed was a bathroom. The light flicked on and I was able to see that it was not some apartment, but a very expensive condo. The bed was very high, with an elaborate headboard and silk bedding. The room was spacious, but what caught my eye was the very timid woman in the bathroom, crying while looking straight ahead.

I walked over to her, to confirm if she were me or someone else. At first glance, I had to gasp and take a step back. It was me, but almost unrecognizable. My blond, not natural brunette, hair was thin and lifeless. My eyes had black circles around them, and the hazel color was dull and almost colorless. I was skinny, but more anorexic than fit. What had gone wrong? God, please tell me what happened?

I looked at the reflection and received a rush of memories. I needed to be careful about what I wished for. My father loaned Alex money for school, and Alex worked for my father while he finished his degree in accounting. He became a very highly valued accountant, at one of the top financial firms. Alex made it very clear that he was not ready for a family, so we focused on our careers and building the life that we wanted. I finished my pre-med degree, then applied for medical school. Alex had an idea of how our future would be shaped, so I decided to assist Alex with his career and quit school to become a medical assistant.

Alex kept moving up in the world, and I was the perfect girlfriend. Things were going great, until we became pregnant. I was afraid that he would be upset with me and sure enough, after I told him that I was pregnant, he silently stared at me for some time and then walked away. He came home after work the day after and brought with him two dozen red roses, a dozen Chinese Stargazer lilies, my favorite flower, and an engagement ring that looked like it weighed twenty pounds.

He told me that he was in a state of shock, and needed time to process the news. I didn't ask if he was happy about becoming a dad; I simply accepted his explanation and left things alone. After I had our child, a son, we married in a very lavish and expensive wedding at my parents' estate, it was like a dream.

Life was perfect for the first few months, falling into a routine, when I found myself pregnant again. Before I could share the news with family, I had a miscarriage. Although Alex was elated that we were not going to have another child, he still blamed me. He became enraged and so frightening. He punched a hole in the wall next to my head, so I left with Caden, to go stay with my parents. He blamed me for his stress, he blamed me for having Caden, for not being able to carry another child to term, and most of all, he blamed me for making him angry enough to want to harm me. Eventually, I went back home. He apologized, but before giving me the chance to accept or reject it, he began kissing me and pulling at my clothes. I yelled at him to stop and pushed him away. He gave me a menacing look and turned to walk away. He took a few steps and took a deep breath. I watched him very closely, in case I had to defend myself but all he did was turn back to face me, apologize, and walk out the room. I let out the breath that I was holding and stood there, thinking about life, and how I had gotten to that point. In college, he was driven and focused on his studies, and didn't go out drinking like the rest of the college population. He would have a drink maybe once or twice a year. He was always gentle with me. My father was a good mentor because I saw the changes in him, from all the time they spent together. They say that women look for men that remind her of her father. Well, Alex was great before working with my dad, and then he became like my father and was perfect for me. I don't know what happened, but he began to revert to the ways of his own father. I was afraid for my life. When he woke later that day, he acted as if he didn't remember what happened between us and requested that I cook him a meal, which I obediently obliged.

Things changed drastically after that day. Although he never hit me after that first time, and he seemed to be able to control his anger around me, I could tell that his attention was no longer on me and I feared for our marriage. He would work late and come home reeking of alcohol. I would smell women's perfume on him, and if I were to question him, he would tell me to mind my own business. I learned not to question him, and to blend into the background and try not to be seen.

Allowing the memories to fade to the background, I couldn't help but cry with myself as we stared at our reflection in the mirror. How had I endured all of that, and still look sane? Why was I still here? Alex controlled the money, but where were my parents? I gasped as another memory hit me. After he hit me, I called my mother for help. I stayed with them and she told me she would take care of it. She only told my father, and persuaded me to go back and fix my marriage for the sake of our child. My tears came faster. I wanted to give myself a hug and tell her it would be okay. Before another thought, the door below slammed and the other me began to panic and tried to fix her face. Wiping away the drying blood, and covering the new bruises with makeup. The bedroom door flew open, everything was silent. Alex walked in and began to speak in a menacing tone, "I thought I told you to fix yourself up before I returned." Almost immediately you could smell the alcohol from his breath. I saw myself backing away from him. I placed myself in between them, facing Alex, hoping that my presence would do something. Alex just went through me and I heard the other me stuttering, "I...I...I..." Before I even turned around to the scene, the other me was already on the floor in the fetal position and Alex was kicking her repeatedly. "Stop! Stop it, Alex! You're killing her... me!!!" I shouted at the top of my lungs, but wasn't heard. I felt powerless. The other me was bleeding from open wounds everywhere. She stopped reacting to his kicks and Alex instinctively bent down to check her pulse. He found that she was still breathing, so he stood up and walked out of the room mumbling, "Where are you, you little shit?"

At first, I didn't understand why he'd mumbled what he'd said, but then it occurred to me, Caden. Fear crept up in me because I had a feeling he was up to no good. I looked at myself, crumpled up on the ground. "Get up!" I shouted, but it was no use, she couldn't hear me. When did I become this person? Just as I was kneeling to the other me, more memories began to come.

I rarely left the house without Caden. This was a rare moment where I left Caden with my mother while I ran errands. I returned home with my purchases but found the house to be very silent and my mother's car gone. I called her and she told me that Alex came home early from wherever he had been, and told her it was okay to leave. It was late afternoon, so I knew that Caden had to be napping in his room. Since there still was no sign of Alex, I decided to go in and check on Caden. Fast asleep, I walked over to give him a little kiss and hug. Bending down for a kiss, I noticed a bruise forming on his left cheek. I quickly rose to panic and started inspecting other parts of his body. He had other bruises forming, and some old ones fading. I tried not to question Alex, but recently, whenever Alex was alone with Caden, my baby always had some sort of accident. He's three, so I took the explanations from Alex, and treated it as boys will be boys, not thinking to ask Caden.

In my frantic search, I woke a very sore Caden. "Mommy, that hurts." My heart broke when I heard his tiny voice. With a shaky voice I asked, "Cay, what happened? Why so many boo-boos?" Caden looked around and relaxed when he finds we are alone, but remained silent. I tried again, "Baby, you can tell me anything. I would never hurt you. But I need to know what happened, so that I can protect you so that you don't get hurt again." His lower lip trembled as he whispered, "Daddy." My heart leapt to my throat and I stood there in disbelief. "Cay, Daddy gave you the boo-boos?" He nodded. I was speechless but knew I needed to reassure him. "Don't worry, baby. You rest and I will fix this. Daddy won't hurt you again." It turned out that Alex was right outside the door, so when I left Caden's room, I was grabbed and dragged to our bedroom. I feared that I knew too much. Apparently, he had been secretly taking his anger out on our child. How did I not see what he was doing? What kind of parent was I, to allow this to go on and not catch on sooner? I was filled with self-hate and tears filled my eyes.

I am brought out of the memory by tiny footsteps. The other me is starting to come to when she hears little Caden's voice, "Mommy, are you okay? Daddy gave you boo-boos like me." She rose up on her knees and took her son into her embrace. In the distance, I heard Alex yelling for Caden to come out. My heart was beating out of my chest, and before I could see Caden and my fate, the room began to fade and I found myself shouting, "NOOOOOOO!"

I WAS STILL SHOUTING when I realized that I was back in Harry's sitting room, sitting up, and scaring Harry to death. I was hyperventilating and fighting an invisible demon. "Emma, Ms. Emma. You are back. Please calm down. It's over." I stopped screaming and fighting, but my heart continued to race. I was feeling all type of emotions and didn't know how to deal with them. I was angry at Alex, sad for the other me, and happy to be back to my reality. Then I realized that I needed to know what happened. "Harry. Please, you have to tell me what happened. I need to know." Harry sat back in his chair. "Ms. Em, I won't be able to do that. You see, I don't have the knowledge of which alternate universe you saw. You can give me details, but it won't make a difference because there is an infinite number of futures. Do you understand?" I did understand, but I didn't like the answer. I nodded and relaxed on the couch. I willed my heart to calm. It was a frightening thought, that I could be living some life being abused. I was so thankful that Greg didn't abuse me. "I think I died, Harry. It was awful! And Caden... what of Caden. My baby!"

Harry grabbed my hands to comfort me. "Sweet child, I told you that you would never experience your own death.

Don't think of what could have been, and be thankful that is not the life you will find yourself living." I looked at him, and for the first time since coming out of the vision, I saw the concern for me in his eyes. "Well, I may not have died in that moment, but I think I may have died sometime after. Caden... Poor Caden. Who would have protected him? I just wish I knew if I got strong or not, at least for Caden."

Harry's face went slack with sadness. "Ms. Em, I may not be able to tell you what happened next in that life but I can tell you, if something was going to change the course of that life, you would have been shown a glimpse. Your current thought path for that alternate you is probably pretty accurate. I'm so sorry." I felt my sadness deepen, but knew there was nothing I could do about it, so I elected to put it past me and move on with the next assignment. I blinked back tears, gave a small smile and willed my voice to be steady and strong, "So, Greg's next, right?" He patted my hands before releasing them. "If you are ready, we will proceed." I nodded.

"Okay, close your eyes. Now, Greg is your current boyfriend, so there will be no need to see the present as we are already there. No need to see the past, because there is no decision to see differently, to change the course of your future. But as I told you before, I am throwing Greg in as a bonus. You have been wonderful company, and I am so glad we've met. Always remember that this does not have to be your future, there are many different outcomes you can find yourself in. After you view this version of a future with Greg, I want you to keep in mind the purpose of all this. It was for you to learn from your past, the present, and possible futures, to help you do what's best for you. Godspeed." Harry was speaking like I was not coming back, or would not see him again. But before I could speak or ponder more on the subject, the darkness of my eyelids changed and a new scene began to form when I opened my eyes.

Chapter Seven

GREG

I OPENED MY EYES AND SAW A BEAUTIFUL SITTING ROOM. It was furnished the way I would like it: simple, contemporary, and colorful. I saw the walls adorned with many pictures, all professionally taken. My parents looked happy, almost too happy. I saw my wedding pictures. I looked almost the same, so I'm guessing that I went along with getting married on the timeline that Greg wanted. There were pictures of our friends at hospital and law firm events. I had pictures up of me becoming head of Pediatric surgery at Handley Medical. I even saw a picture of Lyn and a young boy that looked... too much... like... Greg. My heart sank to the floor. There was a picture, publicly displayed, of my best friend and a small child that looks like my husband. I began to panic. I hope that I had a son and Lyn was like the godmother, sharing a moment with my son. My brain was telling me that I was wrong, but my heart refused to listen. I scanned all the photos and did not find one picture of me and that little boy, or any other children I may have had, for that matter.

I saw myself aging in the photos, so I had to be well over the age of 35. I tried to make memories come. Hello... God, are you there? Nothing. It came easy to me when I was viewing an alternate future with Alex, but no matter how much I tried, I saw nothing. I have to remember what Harry said. Every experience will be different. But it still sucked!

"Where are you going this time? Are you going to be with her again?" It was me. I could hear Greg sigh. I followed the voices. He started speaking, "No, Em..." He sighed again. "You know what? Yes. I am going to see Lyn and my son! Are you happy, now?" I walked up a flight of stairs and into a room where I was sitting on a very lavish bed and Greg was in the walk-in closet, picking out something to wear. "Oh yes, I am very happy for you. Why don't you just leave and be with her. I'm not going to stop you." Greg came out of the closet and approached the possible future me. "Em, you know I can't do that. I would get cut out of your inheritance and lose everything I worked so hard to build."

The future me stood up and smiled, "Oh yeah, I forgot you married me for my money, and a divorce would just ruin you. We wouldn't want to do that." It was said with such sarcasm. She let out a devious laugh. Greg walked out of the closet, once again standing only inches away from her face.

"No, I married you because no one else wanted you. Your father paid me to be with you, you know? He wanted me to push you in all the right directions, to get you to where you are and in the middle of all that, I decided that marrying you would ensure the checks kept coming." Tears started to stream down her face. "That's not true. My father would never do something so hurtful to his only child."

It was Greg's turn to laugh. "Oh, he would, and he did. He told me that he did not want his legacy to end with a doctor who works for free in the poorest neighborhoods, or in any third world countries. He said, and I quote, 'I'm one of the top neurosurgeons in the Goddamned world and I refuse to have my name or DNA attached to some rundown, disease-ridden, Godforsaken free clinic. I don't care if it is her dream. My dream is bigger!' So you see, that's when I stepped in, and here we are now."

I couldn't believe my ears. Had my father really said those things, or was it something said in an alternate past? That thought alone confused me, but I knew that once I returned, I would find out for sure. The other me stood there crying and Greg did nothing to soothe her. I could feel that my parents were gone, so the fact that she couldn't go ask my dad was causing more pain than the words themselves. My father was overly ambitious and always tried to persuade me to be more like him. I wanted to help people, and thought that the best way was to help those who could not help themselves. On some level, I believed Greg when he said that he only married me for the money. He had always been greedy, wanting the next best thing, or the next position up on the corporate ladder. I didn't know how he'd climbed so fast, and now I know that he had help along the way. I guess I can thank my dad for that.

I looked back at myself and felt some memories come my way. The first one was of the very night I met Harry. In this reality, I didn't meet Harry. I went right into Max's and Greg announced our engagement and summer wedding. I just smiled and went along with everything. Lyn was a very supportive friend. She celebrated with me and told me she would be my maid of honor. Life just went along as Greg had planned. We married in June. I finished my residency two years later, and began in the Pediatrics department at Handley. Four years after that, I became the head pediatric surgeon. Greg never once talked about children with me. He worked his way up, and pushed me up the ladder. My parents were ever supportive, but my mother yearned for grandchildren, which I never gave her before she passed away from heart disease. My father became increasingly depressed and lost his mind to Alzheimer's. He was still alive, but a shell of the man he once was.

Greg was very secretive about Lyn for the first few years of our marriage, but once she became pregnant with their son, he basically forced me to accept them both, and accept my life as it was. This fact angered me. How did I become so compliant? I know I let people make decisions for me, but I have never let someone rule my life so much that I didn't benefit from it. Then it hit me. I was afraid of being alone, and afraid of being the only one to make decisions in my life, out of fear of being wrong. I kept him in my life so that I would always have someone to blame for all the wrong in my life when, in fact, my non-participation created the wrong and drama in my life. I had so many achievements in my life. I bypassed my dreams for the dreams of others, and even with the success, I had nothing to show for it. I think that me and the other me reached the realization at the same time. The look on her face said exactly what I was thinking.

"You know what, Greg!? Screw you and my father!!! My father may not have wanted his DNA to be associated with the poor, but his desires should not have overpowered my dreams." She got up and walked out of the room. Greg just made a sound of disgust and continued dressing. I followed the other me into an office. The office was what my father's office used to look like. A very elaborately carved cherry wood executive corner desk, with a wall to wall bookshelf, and a few filing cabinets. She was moving so fast that I missed some of what she was doing. She wrote a few emails and gathered some documents from a safe kept behind a portrait. She took a seat in the office chair with a pile of papers. I took a closer look and saw that they were divorce papers for Greg and the other me. Wow! I didn't think she had it in her until a moment ago. She must have been planning this, or at least dabbling with the idea of being single again. She appeared to be gathering the nerve to take them to Greg. She sat there with her eyes closed, taking deep breaths.

After about five minutes, she opened her eyes, stood up,

and marched back to the room, with me hot on her trail. Greg was sitting on the bed, putting on his shoes. She walked into the room and threw the papers at him. She stood there, waiting patiently for him to pick them up to read them. I was nervous. I couldn't get the thoughts of Alex and his abuse out of my head. I was worried for the other me. "What is this crap?" Greg finally picked up the stack of papers. He read a few lines then looked up at the other me with bewilderment. "What is this, Em?" She gave a nervous laugh. "Don't be dumb Greg, you're the lawyer. Those are divorce papers, that you will sign, so that I may get a life of my own." Greg crumpled the papers slightly when he balled his fist, "Em, you really think I am going to sign that?" He laughed, "You've got some nerve. Now you want to have some balls and try to get rid of me? Baby, you don't know me. That prenup is not iron-clad, and my stipulations have yet to be met. I will take every-thing that's owed to me, and then some. Look, I am willing to forget this whole mess, if you drop the divorce idea."

He tied his shoe and stood up to walk out of the room. The other me was in the doorway, holding up a memory stick. Greg stopped in his tracks. "You will sign those papers. You see, this here memory stick has years and years of your infidelities, and the DNA results proving you fathered a child outside the marriage three years ago. What was my ONE stipulation in the prenup?" The other me shifted her stance and took an obvious thinking pose, "Oh, yes! If there is proven adultery, you walk away with nothing. So, the prenup may not be ironclad, and I may not have met your conditions, but I made sure that I still had a way of locking you out. Don't think I didn't know about Lyn before we got married." She turned to walk away. "Sign the papers and be gone before I return." She was shaky, but she made it to the front door before the floodgates opened. From the bedroom, I could hear Greg screaming before the scene began to fade.

Chapter Eight

I FOUND MYSELF SITTING IN MY CAR, LISTENING TO THE radio DJ introducing the next song in rotation. The Prince song, "Kiss", started flowing through my speakers. I looked at the time on the dashboard, then to my cell phone to check the date. I was back to where I started, before Harry. I was sitting in my car, debating on if I should go into Max's where I would be forced to ignore my knowledge of Lyn and Greg's relationship, and at the same time, put on a happy face to announce Greg and my upcoming nuptials. Pre-Harry, this was what I considered my most important fork in the road and, post-Harry, I was still shaky on which path I should take. This was very frustrating! Where was Harry when I needed him? What was it he said before my last AUV travel? I had to use what I saw... I had to use the past, the present... Damn! What exactly did he say? I need more time. I need to think a little before moving forward, in any direction. It was still early. I know that Greg would expect me to be prompt, but in my line of work, he wouldn't give my tardiness a second glance. I looked at the clock again. I still had twenty-five minutes. I had to decide on my next course of action, and fast. Since I had time to spare, I decided to pay Harry a visit.

I opened my door and was greeted with an icy gust of wind. I pulled my scarf closer to my ears and closed and locked my door. I took the route to the clock store. After the short walk, I arrived and it was closed, with no sign of life behind the glass doors. I knocked, but no one answered. The display window caught my eye, too. It looked a little different, but because it was still a display of clocks, I couldn't figure out what was different. I put my face close to the glass, to try to get a better glimpse into the store but couldn't see too much into the dark shop. Then I remembered when Harry took me, he had to unlock the shop and turn on the lights.

I took my cell phone out and checked the time. It had to be way after store hours. I blew out a breath in frustration, causing the glass to fog. I needed to see him, so that he could tell me more of what he said and tell me what he meant. I would also love it if he explained how I got back to my car. I don't remember him saying anything about traveling back in time. *Was traveling back part of the deal with AUV travel? Is this my second chance at changing my life, and I am screwing it up?* My head was spinning and I was all of a sudden exhausted. I felt light-headed, as if I hadn't eaten all day. I was in no condition to meet with Greg and celebrate an engagement I wasn't sure I was ready for. Right then and there, on the cold stoop of Harry's store, I decided the best thing to do was to go home and think about everything that had happened to me, get a good night's rest, then tackle everything tomorrow. I walked swiftly back to my car just in time to catch the residual heat. My plan came together quickly. I would call Greg, tell a little white lie about working later than planned, then head home for some R&R.

I arrived home to find everything like I had left it that morning. It was as if no time had passed while I was talking to Harry. I don't know why I expected there to be dust build up, or a change in my decor, as if I somehow altered my present. I took my coat and shoes off and headed into the kitchen. I couldn't comprehend what had happened to me. How much time passed as I traveled? How was he able to manipulate time? I never thought to ask if he was, like, an alien or something Other. Suddenly, I went into a panic. As I thought about all the things I didn't know about the universe, I thought about all the things that could have gone wrong today. *Did something go wrong and that is why I was sent back through time? Harry did say I was visiting alternate universes. Does that count as time travel, if I'm not even traveling through my own time? Wait, I think I did travel through my own time! Was Harry telling me everything honestly?* I looked around my kitchen that overlooked the living room. I didn't see anything suspicious, so I sighed in relief. I needed to be more careful; you just never know what's lurking out there, trying to harm you at every corner. I should know. My best friend is more like a frenemy than BFF. She was lurking, and now she's hurting me in the worst way. I tried to calm my heart that was slowly filling with anger. I guess I was lucky I was spotted by someone who appeared to want to help my life, rather than end it. I turned on my Keurig for some tea, and went to put on some comfy pajamas. The one good thing about winter is the comfortable sleepwear and mugs of hot cocoa or tea. After slipping into my pajamas, I decided to lay down and snuggle up. I thought about each of my past boyfriends. I thought about Bruce, and how I wished him well. Alex, and how I hoped he would get his life together and be the man I remembered him to me, and Jimmy. He was the one guy who I feel got it right, after being so wrong. He was living his life by his own rules, and he was happy with what he had. He was not rich, living in a mansion and married to a model. He was living an average life, that was rich in happiness. That's really all I want.

I remembered my tea and let the thoughts of the past, present, and future take a backseat. I went to the kitchen and added a K-cup for a cup of nice English Breakfast tea. It was too late for caffeine, but it was the greatest-tasting tea in my opinion, and I love drinking it at all times of the day. Greg always frowned upon my tea-drinking habits, telling me, "It's called English BREAKFAST for a reason!" What did he know? He was a decaf coffee drinker, and you know you can't trust those guys. I shook my head, trying to escape from my thoughts of Greg. I was home alone and not subjected to anyone else's opinion. I needed to appreciate this time and think about myself for once. I didn't expect Greg to stop by on his way home from Max's. I knew he was too preoccupied with Lyn to even care that I was home alone, and in need of someone or something to snuggle with. Just thinking about him and Lyn made me so angry. How dare he say I need to wait for children, but he gives her a child almost right away?

I know it hasn't happened, yet, or may never happen. Just the thought of it being a possibility kills me. But I am not as complacent or weak as everyone thinks I am. One thing the future me and the current me have in common is our love for collecting evidence and documenting everything for protection. Greg rarely speaks the truth when it comes to answering me. For the longest, I've been watching, learning, and documenting. I am not a negative person. I don't think that every person will wrong me. I just planned for a rainy day, after the first few instances of suspicion. How does that saying go? "Fool me once, shame on you. Fool me twice, shame on me." I may never get the nerve to speak up and defend myself, but I stopped emotionally investing myself in our relationship after the first few lies about working late. I know I should have spoken up. In that sense, I am weak. After countless attempts throughout the years, I should be strong enough to follow through. I guess in some ways I am passive-aggressive. I'm sure having everyone rule my life has something to do with it. I wanted to please everyone and make everyone happy with me, so much so that I lost my voice along the way. Sadness shadowed me. My mind was exhausted, so I drank the rest of my tea and headed to bed.

Chapter Nine

I woke with a start; so many thoughts running through my head. I grabbed my cell phone off the nightstand and saw that Greg had left a text message: *ok*. Ok, that was all I got after I called him, left a voicemail and text message letting him know that I was working late, had a lot on my mind, and was going home to sleep. He did not even ask to see if I was okay, or needed someone to talk to. I even texted Lyn, giving her the same excuse. She at least texted me back, asking me if I was okay and if I needed to have a girl's night. I declined, of course, but it still made me feel like she, of all people, was being more true to me than the man that wanted to marry me.

I rolled out of bed, feeling like I'd been hit by a car. I felt my dreams still haunting me as I walked to my bathroom. I looked at myself in the mirror. I looked like I'd just completed a 20-hour shift. I thought back to my night. What was it that had me so restless? The deeper I thought, the more the dreams seemed to be moving beyond my grasp. My mind focused on Harry. Everything revolved around Harry. He showed me the past I tried so hard to forget, the present that I am still trying to process, and an alternate universe I never knew existed. I know that I am supposed to use what he showed me to make the right decisions, right now, to benefit my future, but I still don't know the path I should take. I leaned against the bathroom counter. In one hand, I can stay with Greg and change the possible future I saw. I already had the dirt I needed to keep him in line. I could present that to him, get a prenuptial agreement, and be the Stepford wife he's looking for. I would not allow my "best friend" to stay around, although I have dirt on her, too. She may think that she has been careful while getting it on with my fiancé all this time, but she forgets how well I pay attention to routines and my love for a good mystery. I may not have had her followed by a private investigator like I did Greg, but because she was messing with my man, I got two for the price of one. She must think that I don't know her well. I remember she used to go out to the clubs and bars and flaunt her stuff to any guy that looked like he made at least six figures. She had a nose for money. It's been at least a year since she's dragged me out to some ritzy club to scout for a man, and I know that she doesn't have any of those clueless, blinded by beauty, men sniffing around her. The last time I asked her about her love life, she told me she was having a dry spell and was trying to focus on work. I smelled the bull because in all the time I've known her, she has never wanted to support herself. Her attitude has always been, "I'm doing this so that men don't think I'm a gold digger. Once I get a man that will take care of me, I will marry him, quit my job, and pop out a few kids." Why were we even friends? I always knew that we had different ideas on relationships and men. She was just always there for me; the one constant support that I leaned on time after time. She's still there for me when I need her, but she's there for Greg, too, and I am not much for sharing.

I blew out an exaggerated breath and stood on my own two feet. As I walked to the kitchen to put on some coffee, I thought about the life that I would have if I stayed with Greg, on my terms. Could I be happy? On the other hand, I could definitely find someone else and be happy. I would stay away from men that my father had influence over and find myself a nice guy who is looking for a real relationship, built on trust and love and the possibility of having a family together. It shouldn't be hard, but I feel that. with my schedule, it will be a challenge. I retrieved my cup of coffee and sat at the kitchen table.

Today I was going to relax and do something for myself. I was thinking that I would get a manicure and a massage after I went to the Clock shop and spoke to Harry. My eye caught the manila folder sticking out of my pile of mail. I put it there to mask the content. I knew what was in the folder, even if I haven't opened it yet. The day Greg proposed to me, I met with my private investigator, Jeremy, and he gave me the envelope before wishing me luck. I didn't need the investigator, or Harry's AUV travel, to know the Greg was not being true to me. I saw it in his eyes and heard it in some of the jokes he told. He was not fooling anyone, yet, I was the fool for letting him think he was getting away with it. I want to make my father happy and proud of me, but I think that I should be putting a limit as to how far I should go to make that happen. I pulled the envelope out. It was thick, and I wasn't sure I was ready to see the content behind the seal. My gut feeling was one thing, seeing things with my own eyes was another. I tried to think of it like a Band-Aid as I held my breath and tore through the sealed flap. My hands trembled as I lifted the envelope's bottom, and the items slid out onto the table. I couldn't believe the level of detail the investigator included. There were so many pictures, emails, memory disks which I was sure held video. On top of the pile was a typed inventory. I counted fifty-six items. Jeremy went above and beyond, and for that I was grateful. I'm not sure if everything he did and provided was legal, but I wasn't going to tell if he wasn't. My cell phone beeped and I knew that it was 8 am. My schedule this week at the hospital started at 9 am, but today is my off-day. I decided that the contents of my investigation could wait, so I slid everything back into the envelope and put it in my handbag.

After I showered and dressed, I jumped into my car and made my way back to the clock store. It was a little after 9 when I arrived and the store was already open. I walked in and the bell signaled the arrival of a potential customer. I was the only one in the store, but the tick-tock of all the clocks filled the room with sound. I looked around and thought that the store looked very different during the day. I browsed the glass cases as I waited for someone to greet me. Harry may not have heard me, but I hoped he wasn't the only one working today. As I browsed the cases closer to the back left of the store, I noticed a photo of Harry hanging on the wall. He looked the same as I remembered him, with a smile that could warm the coldest of hearts. I smiled up at the portrait as if he could see me. Lost in my thoughts, I didn't hear anyone enter the room. "Uh, Miss. May I help you?" I about jumped out of my skin. "I do apologize, miss. I did not intend to frighten you. I'm Harold, the owner of the shop." With my hand pressed to my chest and my heart beating erratically, I responded, "Oh, it's all right, Harold. I was just admiring this picture of Harry and didn't hear you coming." He sighed, "Oh, my father. Yes. Did you know him?" I found it strange that he referred to Harry in the past-tense. I looked at the photo and back at the newcomer, who had just announced that he was Harry's son. It was then that I saw the resemblance. He looked like a spitting image of Harry, just a bit younger, maybe in his forties. I was being rude just staring at the stranger so I answered. "Yes, I do know him. I'm Emma. Is he around? I must speak with him." A glimpse of sadness crossed his face and I hoped it was not what I thought it meant. He placed his hands on top of mine as if to comfort me, like we were old friends. "I am so sorry to have to tell you like this, but my father passed away five years ago yesterday."

It was like time stopped. The sound of the clocks disappeared. How was this possible? Five years!!! But I had just seen him yesterday. I tried to relax my face because I didn't want to alarm Harold. He was comforting me, thinking I had just found out his father's been dead for five years, and not the fact that I'm freaking out because I saw Harry walking around just yesterday. I lifted a hand out of his grasp and touched his shoulder, "I'm so sorry for your loss." A smile of gratitude came across his face. "Thank you, Emma. My father never mentioned you, but I'm sure that's because he knew so many people." It was my turn to smile, "I'm sure. Your father was very wise and he knew a lot about time. He had a way of making me understand my past, so to move forward in my future." I didn't know what else to say. I couldn't just say: *Hi, your dad took me time traveling and I forgot the major thing he told me to remember, so that I won't screw up my future. Do you know, by chance?* Harold walked over to the portrait and touched it fondly. "My father did believe that there was more to time and clocks than what we relied on them for." He let out a short laugh, "He used to say, 'Time moves forward. If you're not moving with it, you risk staying in the past.' I never really understood what he meant. I used to tell him, 'Dad, we have no choice but to move with time' and he'd wave me off and say that one day I'd understand." I pondered over this for a moment and then I finally understood and in a whisper I declared, "Indecision can cause you to be frozen in time. No personal growth and no goals met." I spoke too low for Harold and he rewarded me with a 'huh?' I looked up at him and smiled, "Harold, your father was right! You can get stuck in the past." He looked at me, confused. As I moved toward the door I spoke again, "I have to go, but it was nice meeting you, Harold." I was out the door before he spoke another word.

I went to my car and was ready for what was in the manila envelope. Harry was a brilliant man. He showed me that if I didn't change the way my life was going, I would continuously repeat the same mistakes, which ultimately meant I would be stuck in the past. But if I freed myself, I would move forward with time. I pulled the envelope from my handbag and opened it up. I browsed the pictures and, surprisingly, I had no reaction to them. Most of them were of Lyn, but there were a few of women I had never seen before, which was a surprise to me. Each item had a timestamp. Jeremy had placed everything in chronological order. For that, he deserved a bonus.

As I made a mental note to send Jeremy a bonus check, I looked at a few emails between Greg and Lyn. That dirty bitch! She was telling Greg all my secrets, that she told me would never leave her lips, and she was plotting against me. She and Greg were going to try and take my inheritance, plus the money that my father has promised him, and keep me in the dark. The emails were like love letters and I doubt Greg loved either of us. There were phone call transcripts that ranged from casual to sexual. Jeremy included the conversations on the memory cards, as well. Lyn did things to Greg that I thought were even beneath her. I couldn't believe that a woman would degrade herself just for a man with money, correction, a man dating a woman with money. After reviewing the photos, phone transcripts, credit card receipts, and medical records, I had my mind made up. I was not going to put myself in a position of unhappiness for my father. The fact that I had evidence of my father trying to pay Greg off would be enough to secure my father's word that he would never interfere with my life again. So many people I trusted, and they all screwed me over. The tears started forming in my eyes, just as my stomach began to rumble. I laughed because my stomach helped hold the tears back. I would not shed a tear for them. I would get even.

I decided against going straight to get a manicure and massage. I, instead, elected to go to that coffee shop that Harry took me to. I got out of the car, pulling my scarf closer to my ears, and walked to the coffee shop. It was called Jackpot and they had really good tea, at least I hoped it wasn't my imagination telling me that they did. I opened the door and the shop was fairly empty, which I was happy about. I went over to the counter and ordered a tea and one of their house special sandwiches. As I tried to wrap my mind around Harry and his existence or non-existence last night, I felt that if he was right about time, then he would be right about the Jackpot coffee shop. I took a table in the corner, the same table that Harry and I had sat at just last night. I thought about what I was going to do to get even with those who I love and thought loved me. My father was easy. I would see him at Sunday brunch, show him the phone transcript between him and Greg, tell him I have the recording, too, then kindly tell him if he interferes with my life again, I will tell Mom all his secrets. He knows me well enough to know that I know what goes on during those late nights at the hospital. That will be our truce. Since I don't need a truce with Lyn or Greg, I needed to get them good, and make it hurt.

As I silently plotted my revenge, I heard someone clear their throat. "Hello, earth to Emma. You there, or have the long hours at the hospital taken you hostage?" I looked up and saw the sunlight shining on this man's face. It was an angel talking to me. He had sandy blond hair, greenish hazel eyes, and a smile with matching dimples to die for. Were angels blond? I didn't care. My eyes continued to move lower as I spotted a glimpse of toned, tanned muscles. The angel sat down in front of me and the light moved from his face and I saw who it was. I straightened up and hoped I wasn't drooling. Harry messed up my brain. I didn't know the difference between what was real and fantasy. This man was definitely fantasy, because I used to fantasize about him all through med school. "Uh... Hi... How are you?"

I couldn't get my brain to work. What was his name? Why couldn't I remember his name? He was only in my dreams for years. "Charlie. The name's Charlie Jacqner. I thought you'd at least remember my name. After all, we were lab partners for the whole entire first year in med school. We even had classes together every year after." I put my head in my hands. I was a complete idiot. "I'm so, so sorry. I remember you. I'm just... I'm having a bad day." He smiled, "Already? It's still morning." He turned his lips upside down to try to look sad. I remembered, now, why I was so infatuated with him. "I brought you your sandwich. It's on the house, so I hope that it brightens your day a tiny bit." I looked down at the table as he sat the plate down in front of me. "I brought your favorite tea; English Breakfast." He remembered my favorite tea. I stared down at my plate and at the tea, and frowned as the tears started forming again. Why didn't he and I ever get together? He'd always been so nice to me. I pushed the tears back just as Charlie touched my arm. "I can take the tea back if you don't want it. I just thought..." He let the last sentence linger. I smiled, "Charlie, it's great! Thank you so much for remembering me and remembering my favorite tea." He smiled and got up to leave when a thought hit me. "Wait!" He turned and waited. "Why did you bring me my favorite tea? I mean, what happened to becoming a doctor? I know you graduated." I blushed. He did not attend graduation, but I had one of my dad's contacts look into his file. He came and sat down again, smiling that beautiful smile. "I did graduate and I am a doctor." I looked at him, confused and he laughed. "This is Jackpot. Get it, Jacqner... Jackpot. My family owns this place. I have part ownership of this place and I like to come down and work on my days off at County." It all made sense and I think he recognized the moment when I understood. I was envious of him. He seemed so happy and I wanted what he had. He was really giving back, working at County. That was something that I wanted to do. He was looking at me, waiting for a reply. "That makes perfect sense. I don't know how I couldn't have gotten it sooner." I was embarrassed so I laughed. He once again got up and proceeded to leave. "Well, Emma, let me know if I can get you anything else." I nodded and went back to my tea. I wanted him to stay, I wanted him to want me. I am sure that I lost my chance with him. My father and his minions have always caused me trouble, but it was all going to end. I ate my whole sandwich and drank my tea. Harry was not lying when he said that the food here was great. Charlie and his family knew how to please the palate. I wondered what else Charlie could please. I shook my head at my dirty thoughts. I had plenty of time later to fantasize about him. Right now, I needed to clear my present, to make way for my future.

I gathered my things and made my way to the counter. Charlie whispered to the girl at the counter and she promptly left and went to the back. I made my way to the counter and pulled my wallet out of my bag. "Charlie, you have to let me pay for my meal. It was delicious." He held up his hands to wave me off. "Emma, please, it was my treat. Plus, the owner owes me for a few favors." We both laughed. I put my wallet back in my bag, "Thank you. It was so nice to see you, Charlie. Bye." I turned to leave and just as I was opening the door, Charlie was behind me, "Emma, I'm probably out of place, but would you like to go out sometime?" I couldn't believe it. Charlie was asking me out. My heart was singing yes but I knew that if I started dating him now, I would be pulling him into my mess. I smiled again, "I'd love to go out with you, but my life is a mess right now. I would want to start things right with you." He looked defeated but still managed a smile. "I understand. It was just an impulse. I couldn't see you again and not say something." I didn't want to rehash the past, so I just smiled and nodded. "Look, when I get my life back on track and if you're still single, I'll come looking for you." He nodded and opened the door for me. It was one of the hardest things I ever had to walk away from, but I knew that if I didn't set my life straight, I would get stuck in the past.

Chapter Ten

I SLOWLY WALKED TO MY FRONT DOOR, HEART POUNDING out of my chest. I tried to fit the key into my lock but my hands would not stop shaking. Everything happened so fast. I put my back to my door and took a few deep breaths. My mind was swimming and I needed to process everything before it made me go crazy. I turned and faced the door. My first task, open the front door. With less shaky hands, I finally fit the key with the lock and opened the door. I quickly entered my townhouse and locked myself in. It had been a whirlwind of events. I stripped off my coat, boots, and jeans as I walked through the foyer. I didn't care where they landed, I just needed to get into something more comfortable. I went into my bedroom and put on a pair of my college sweatpants. I was finally able to relax, so I sighed and fell back onto my bed. As I laid there, my shock started to wane. I was finally able to process the events of the day.

After I regretfully left Charlie at the Jackpot, I took care of myself and had that massage and manicure. The whole time I was trying to relax, Greg called and texted me. It was not like he was concerned about me. The tone I felt was more like anger and frustration from me ignoring him. I wish I could turn my phone off, but I gave my personal cell number out to some of my favorite patients, in case of emergency. I had to clear my head and talking to him would only make me go back on what I had decided to do. I was going to call it off. I needed to see who I was, without the influence of my father, and since Greg was my father's lackey, I needed to be rid of him, as well. He didn't help his defense by cheating on me with my best friend. After I finished with my pampering, I was frustrated by the constant vibrating of my phone. I looked at my screen and saw that I had 25 missed calls, all from Greg, and 5 voicemail message. I listened to the messages. In the first one, he sounded a bit concerned. "Hey baby, where are you? I've been trying to reach you. Please call me so that I know you are okay. Okay. Love you." He never sounded that sweet, which led me to believe he had done something last night, and he thought I knew about it. As the messages played on, his voice got increasingly angry, until the sweetness disappeared completely. The last message almost shocked me... almost. "Emma. Listen here, you better call me, or lord knows what I'll do. Why are you acting this way? Why the fuck are you ignoring my calls? I will not tolerate this nonsense after we're married. FUCK!!!!..." I had to listen to that one again and after the second time, I heard what I was looking for. He called me a bitch. It was low and clipped, when he hung up the phone, but there it was. I sat in my car and willed myself not to cry. My tears won because I sat there and cried for almost 15 minutes. I glanced at my passenger seat and saw the manila envelope. When I saw it, my tears dried up quick. I remembered that I didn't have to put up with his mess. I was over being used, abused, and walked all over. I needed to take back my life.

I started the car and decided that I was going to pay Greg a visit and confront him. I wanted to get this over and done with, as soon as possible. I had to get past any hurt and pain so that I could get on with my life, before I got too old and ended up having kids at 35, anyway. I decided against calling him before making my way to his house. He owned a year old modest colonial-style home, with a pool and guest house. He said that he was waiting for us to be married before he went for the house on the hill, with a mile-long driveway and a gate that kept all outsiders away. I thought the house he owned was perfectly fine, but for men like him and my father, bigger is always better. Everyone wondered why we never lived together. I never thought about it before, but now I know that it was probably so that he could be with Lyn any time he wanted, without me being in the way. Jerk!

I arrived at his house and to my surprise, I saw Lyn's car. I thought that Greg would be more discreet, but at the same time, he didn't expect me to just show up. I mean, I have always called first, so this is out of the ordinary for me.

Maybe Lyn was concerned about me after Greg called her when I didn't answer his call. That may redeem her, but I would need to feel her apology when she apologized about sleeping with my man behind my back. I wondered what she would have to say about her actions. I'd seen her be remorseful, and I'd seen her bitch-ness at its highest. I'll just have to see when I get in there. I went over and touched Lyn's car, cold. She had been here a while and something tells me that she may have even been here overnight.

I shook my head and tried not to think the worst, which was probably the closest to the truth. I took the short walk to the front door. The house was a little different from most houses. The kitchen was the first room of the house when you walked through the front door. I'm not sure why Greg bought a house so strange, but he hated it, so he always used the side door, which opened to the sitting area right before the living room. The side door was located in the garage, which was currently closed, so I had no other way to get in but the front door.

I grabbed the key that is always kept in the hide-a-key rock near the porch. I unlocked the door and walked in, shutting the door behind me. It was silent, almost too quiet. Maybe I was wrong. Maybe Lyn did come over here after Greg called her and they both went out looking for me. My heart softened a bit just thinking about that. Just as I was opening the swinging door that separated the kitchen and the living room, I heard Lyn laughing. I stopped and held my breath. "Stop it, Greg! This is serious. What if she comes to your house? She can't see us like this." Greg snorted. "She would never come by without calling first. That was my first rule when we started dating, and she has yet to break it. Trust me, we have time." He paused for a moment, "See, she hasn't called or texted yet." They kiss and I heard the ruffle of clothes and some moaning from Lyn. I felt the bile rise in my throat. How could they be getting it on while I'm out there, possibly lost or kidnapped? What horrible people! I took a deep breath. It was now or never. I walked into the room and looked around. I didn't see anyone at first, then I heard moaning again but this time from Greg. I went in the direction of the noise and found myself standing behind the couch. Lyn and Greg were intertwined together on the couch. I felt the anger building within myself. I had to remind myself that I had a purpose and my anger would only change the direction of my mission. I took a silent deep breath, then cleared my throat. "I'm sorry. Am I interrupting something?" Lyn opened her eyes when she heard me begin to speak. She pushed Greg off her and sat up to try to button her shirt, "Em, umm... I can explain." Greg pushed off the couch and tried to pull up his pants. "Em, what are you doing here? You haven't been answering my calls or text messages, and then you just show up at my place! What the hell has gotten into you?" Just like him to try to push this off on me and dismiss the fact that he just pulled his penis out of my best friend's vagina. Rich! Just as Greg got off the couch, Lyn was rounding the couch trying to neutralize the situation. "Em, let me explain. See, when you didn't show last night, Greg got really drunk and so I stayed and drank with him and..."

Greg turned bright red, "Shut up, Lyn! You shut your mouth right now." I looked at Greg and back to Lyn, who was still talking. "...we just talked all night until Max's closed. We walked to our cars, and--"

Not wanting to hear the rest, Greg and I both shouted "Shut up, Lyn!" I glared at Greg for stealing my moment, then decided to take control of this discussion. "Lyn, Greg may think he had me fooled, but I've known you since high school. Did you really think I didn't know? There is nothing you can say about this whole moment to make what you did right or okay, even. What do you have to say for yourself? I was supposed to be your best friend." I paused to give her a moment to respond. She looked like she was grasping at straws. "He... He... he propositioned me. I didn't expect to come home with him last night. I would never have done this to you on purpose. You should know that."

Greg threw up his hand, visually expressing my disgust with Lyn's blatant lie. She would most definitely do this to me for the right price. "Lyn, please. You really think I don't know about Greg cheating on me. We haven't had sex in months. I'm not stupid." I looked to Greg to see his reaction. There was some shock, but it cleared when he caught me looking at him. "Yeah, Greg. I knew about Lyn. Question is, does Lyn know about the others?" I turned to Lyn and found her glaring at Greg. "What is she talking about Greg? What others? GIRLS!?"

I covered my mouth to hide my smile. This was hilarious. Lyn thought she was the only one, somehow, or that being the other girl next to her best friend was an acceptable relationship. Delusional wench. "Lyn, you thought Greg was going to leave me for you." I laughed loudly as she looked at me with confusion. "He must not have told you that, as per his agreement with my father, he had to stay happily married to me in order to continue to milk the cash cow. So you see, you were always going to be his dirty little secret."

It was Greg's turn to look surprised. He is thinking *How could she know about my arrangement with her dad.* He was speechless, unbelievable. I decided that I was finished with this conversation, and part of my life. "Lyn, this is my last act of kindness in our friendship. We are no longer friends." I turned to Greg next. "And Greg, the engagement is over. You are free to date Lyn openly." I turned to walk away when I remembered the envelope. I pulled it out of my bag and removed the media items and placed them back into my pocketbook. I turned back around and saw Greg and Lyn comforting each other in an embrace, like they were victims in the whole ordeal. "Oh, and Lyn, I just want to remind you that you said you would never turn into your mother, and here you are. And if you were ever wondering about what Greg's been up to the last six months, here you go." I handed the manila envelope to Lyn's stiff hands. I turned and walked away before either of them could open the envelope or respond.

I opened my eyes and returned to the present, with a full

body chill. I can't believe I was finished with Greg and Lyn. I can't believe that I found them in mid-sexual relations. I shivered. That was the nastiest thing I have ever seen, and I wish I could erase it from my memory. Since I told Greg I knew about his deal with my father, I was sure that I would be receiving a call from my dad any moment now. He was going to try to silence me, or maybe yell at me for breaking it off with Greg. Whatever position he comes at me from, I am ready to face him.

I decided to get up and use my kitchen for the first time in a week. I went to the freezer and grabbed one of those frozen meals. I wasn't actually going to cook. I'm not really into cooking but I sure know how to use my microwave. I decided that a cup of tea would be nice, as well, so I turned on the Keurig. Before my meal was complete, I heard my cell phone ringing. Here we go. The phone rang for a third time before I reached it. I looked at the caller ID, my dad. I picked up with my most cheerful voice, "Hey, Dad!"

"Hey, baby girl. What's this I hear about you breaking it off with Greg?" Just like my dad to get right to the point. It made me wonder how he did his job as head of cardiology, with tact like that. I tried to match my dad's tone and direction, "Who told you that?"

"Well, Greg called me, upset, and told me that, out of nowhere, you called off the engagement." Now I was upset. "Did he also tell you that he was sleeping with Lyn, and some other women I don't even know?" He sighed. "I don't know about any of that. He's a good man, sweetie. Why don't you think on it a few days and make up?" I scoffed. "Dad, he is not a good man. If he was, he would not need to be paid to be with me." He was silent, so I continued, "Dad, I would rather live a lonely life, than be with someone my father is paying to be with his only daughter. I am not an invalid. I can make my own decisions about my life and my relationships. I don't need a push in the right direction, and your dreams do not override my dreams for my life. If you're worried about your DNA being connected to something you feel is beneath you, I will change my name so that you don't have to feel shame because of your only child." He sighed again. "Em, baby, I just wanted the best for you. You deserve the best in life. You're --"

"Dad," I stopped him. "I deserve the right to make my own decisions and if that's not enough for you, then I'm sorry." I don't know where all this courage was coming from, but I was happy for the strength. "Em, just think about it, okay? Your mom would be heartbroken if she heard this news." Now he was trying to use my mother's happiness to sway me into doing what he wanted. I was livid. "Dad, you just don't understand. I'm just wasting my breath. Tell Mom I'm sorry that I won't be making it to Sunday brunch for a while." I hung up just as my dad was responding. I couldn't stay on the phone for another moment.

I felt tears running down my face before I was full-on crying. Why couldn't my father understand that I needed to make my own happiness? I cried for myself, and for the presents and futures of all my past boyfriends. I felt for Alex the most. He had such a bright future, and it all crumbled because of greed. I just wish there was something I could do to help him. I saw my future with Greg, and it was not happy. There was no love, or even children or pets for me to love. I couldn't let that happen to myself, especially after I saw my possible future with Bruce. There was some tragedy, but a lot of love to make up for it. Bruce would have loved me for who I was, and loved me through all of our misfortunes. Even my future with Jimmy wasn't horrible. We had love and family, that was enough for me. My parents may not have felt I did all the right things, but it all felt right because I was happy. Jimmy was wrong from the start. Although a possible future with him could have been acceptable, I think that it was something I am glad I didn't take a chance on. We had love and family, but I think eventually I would have felt some regret for not following my dreams in going to medical school.

I got a small glimpse into what my life should be like and I needed to have it. One thing I learned from seeing possible futures is that I can never erase the past. Those futures were all possibilities but not guarantees, not for this version of me anyway. I am who I am because of the experiences of my past and present and without my experiences, I may not have ever reached the positive outcomes I saw in those visions. It all made me long for things to change in my life. I may wish for the future I saw with Bruce, but I am glad he found the woman he will spend the rest of his life with. I think that he was one of the best things I had in my life, maybe even the only person who tried to get me to live my own life, and one day I will thank him. I wish Harry were here. I wish I could thank him for showing me how to take back my life and find my own happiness, even if I wasn't sure yet what that meant. My thoughts drift to Charlie. I want to see him again but I think that I should focus on myself, and what it means to be happy.

Chapter Eleven

CHARLIE

It has been exactly two months to the day since Harry walked in and out of my life. I will never forget the effect he had on me. My life had found a new rhythm, and I felt like life had just begun. I felt free and strong, like I could conquer the world. I took each day one at a time, and savored each minute.

I left my townhouse late afternoon, still feeling like a new me. I decided that I'd go out for an early dinner before calling it a day, in preparation for tomorrow's shift. Life has been going well for me. My father and I made peace and we continued our Sunday brunch, after not speaking for a few weeks. He says it's to keep my mother happy but I know that he is trying to make amends. He's so transparent, now that I took my blinders off. My mother had no clue about any of the events that occurred. All she knew is that I was no longer with Greg, and that I was happy.

I loved my mom for being uncomplicated. She was happy, as long as she believed I was happy. My father was worried that she would have a breakdown after the news of my breakup but she confided in me, saying she thought something was off about him and that she just couldn't put her finger on it. She named a few things she considered "off," all having to do with his pedigree, but even if she knew about all the things he did, I don't think she would comment about it. They were too risqué for her taste. I wish her eyes were opened to the things that my father did, but something tells me she already knows and accepted it to keep the peace. Always the peacemaker, my mother. I could easily see my future when I look at her. Never speaking out of turn, always giving and never taking what's deserved. I almost became my mother, but I feel my life would have been a lot worse with Greg.

The AUV traveling helped me grow a pair. At first, I thought I would feel some sort of remorse or sadness after I stuck it to Greg but, surprisingly, I was okay with him not being in my life the moment I walked out of his house. It took me a minute to shake the initial shock but once it was gone, it was as if Greg and I were never together. I actually ran into him at Max's while I was out with some co-workers one night. He was alone at the bar and looked horrible, like he hadn't slept in days. I guess Lyn didn't want anything to do with him, after she found out that he was sleeping around on her, too. As a matter of fact, I heard she was the one who told the partners at his law firm about him getting paid to marry me, and trying to con me out of my inheritance. The partners looked down on his actions, saying it was unethical, and wondered where else he was performing unethically. They decided to begin an investigation into his career. They uncovered a few cases where Greg violated the ABA Model rules. Although there wasn't a significant number of cases handled unethically, the firm fired him for taking bribes. There is still no word on his disbarment, but he was very fortunate that he wasn't prosecuted. He could be in jail for the things he did, yet, he's out free but something tells me that he placed himself in a prison of his own making. He will never be a partner for any reputable law firm, and because of the media coverage, may never live the lifestyle he always felt he deserved. So when I saw him, I simply looked at him, wondering what I had found attractive in him and continued my conversation with my new circle of friends. I was numb toward my past with Greg, and was ready to move forward with my life.

I found myself back near JackPot. During the past two months, I did nothing but think about Charlie. I wondered if he found someone, or if we could ever make it work. I forced myself to stay away from this area, in fear of running into him. I just couldn't bear it if he found someone else. What would I say to him? I used the last two months for myself, to learn about all the things that make and would make me happy. I decided to continue my training at Handley. I am sure that is the one and only reason my father started talking to me again. I'm sure he's saying, 'At least she's not throwing her career down the drain.' I realized that I am being helpful, wherever I work, especially if I am working with children, and that made me happy. My stomach growled so I turned off the ignition, left my car, and began to walk toward the shop. I was nervous but I told myself, no matter what, I will not ask him out. If he still wanted to go out, he would hope-fully ask me again.

I took a deep breath before I opened the door. It was about 5 PM on a Friday evening and Jackpot was fairly busy for a coffee shop. I quickly made my way to the end of the line and looked around for Charlie. He was nowhere around. When it was my turn to order, I ordered the house special sandwich and a hot tea. Surprisingly, the table that I now think of as 'my' table was free, so I took it. I continued to look around but was not having any luck. I decided to ask the server when he brought my food. "Here you are, house special and a black tea. Will you be needing anything else?" I looked over my food, then back to the server. He was a teenager, about 16 or 17 years old. He had shaggy black hair, brown eyes, and a concert tee hidden underneath his apron. "Ummm, no. Thank you." He turned to walk away and I found the courage to ask, "Wait. There is one thing. Is Charlie around?" He quickly answered, like I was asking him about the specials, "Naw. He doesn't really work here. He just pops up whenever he's not working his real job." Without waiting for a follow-up, the boy made his exit. I sat there and ate my sandwich, which was delicious like I remembered but once it was gone, I was left with disappointment. I wasn't sure why I thought he was going to be there. I knew he was a doctor at County and worked long hours like I did. I guess I got my hopes up, once I felt I was ready for a new relationship. Why didn't we exchange phone numbers? I was so dumb! I felt like showing up at his job was a bit like stalking, so I decided that I would just try my luck at JackPot and hope that he's here one of the days I visit.

My life again went into a different but comfortable rhythm. I worked 12-hour shifts, usually Monday through Saturday, always having Sunday off for Sunday brunch with my parents, and a random weekday off each week. My father was still influencing that part of my life, but Sunday brunch I didn't mind. I would go out with co-workers whenever enough of us could get the evening off. But the largest change for me was my weekly visits to JackPot for lunch. Although JackPot was not my usual lunch spot, I needed to see Charlie. I needed to know if he and I could ever be. I thought about our past, and what I felt toward Charlie in med school. Charlie and I had an innocent flirtatious friendship in class. He was attractive, and I was attracted to him. I believe he was attracted to me, but I'm not sure why we never took things further. I wasn't with Greg yet, and he and I never discussed a significant other. Still, Charlie never asked me out, so I was curious as to why nothing happened between us and this made me more determined to see him. It was going on six weeks since I first stepped back into JackPot, and I have yet to run into Charlie. I had all but given up. My thought process now was, if we run into each other, great. If not, I will still enjoy the delicious food and comforting environment.

It was again Friday afternoon. I was running late for lunch due to one of my patient's parents worrying about a routine tonsillectomy. I needed to put their minds at ease, and it took almost an hour of talking and explaining before they felt comfortable enough to leave. They were worried about my inexperience but I told them that the senior pediatric surgeon was going to be overseeing the procedure, and their little girl would be in good hands. I had only thirty-five minutes for lunch but I was determined to keep my routine. I took the short drive to JackPot. I usually was a mixture of nervous and excited, at the prospect of seeing Charlie, but this time I was in a hurry. I ran into the shop, ordered my food and sat at MY table. I was reading some email on my smartphone while I waited for my food. I now had twenty-three minutes.

"Your food, Miss. House special and English Breakfast tea." I didn't need to look up to see who it was, Charlie. I looked up and had the biggest, most goofy smile. I was completely giddy. He was everything and sparked every sense. His hair was slightly longer, but his eyes and dimples were still to die for. And if I had died that very moment, I would have been an extremely happy woman. He raised an eyebrow at me, but I couldn't seem to find my voice. How old was I? "Uh, so you're the cute stalker lady that my employees have been telling me about."

My smile dropped and my expression was replaced with

shock and embarrassment. Was it that obvious? I turned beet-red. He laughed and continued, "They said that you came in every Friday afternoon, sat at the same table, ordered the same meal, and ask for me by name. I have to say, I am very flattered." He flashed his smile and I couldn't help but smile. He sat down across from me. "I didn't know it was you until Angie, the cashier, told me, and I quote 'the same girl you were horribly flirting with a couple of months ago.' There was a face to go with my horrible flirting." He let out a laugh. "If I'd known it was you, I would have come sooner. Why have you been coming in here looking for me? There are other ways of finding people." He smiled, but then looked at me, concerned.

I couldn't let him think I was that crazy stalker lady so I had to have a witty response. "First, I wasn't stalking you. I enjoy the house special and since I was coming for lunch anyway, I thought I'd see if you were around." He leaned back in the chair and rubbed his chin, giving a 'hmmm' sound while he digested the information, before responding. "So, you weren't really looking for me for any particular reason?" I leaned in and waved for him to come close as if I had a secret to tell. "You did give me my meal for free. I wanted to see if I could get a repeat service." I said it in a whisper, then winked before sitting straight up to laugh.

He joined in my laughter. "So you were just trying to use me. I see how this relationship is going to be." He continued laughing, but I stopped and looked at him. What did he mean by that? Was he still interested? I looked at my watch and saw that I had exactly seven minutes to get back to the hospital. "Oh, no! I have to go." I stood up and started gathering my things. Charlie also stood, with a perplexed look across his face. "Leaving already? Did I say something wrong?" I looked at him and reached over to touch his cheek. There was a little stubble but I could still feel the smooth skin underneath. I smiled, "Charlie, it's not you. I am going to be late getting back to the hospital and I have a surgery to perform this afternoon." I sighed and started for the door. Before running out, I turned to speak, not wanting to leave him confused about my intent. "I hope to see you same time next week." Then I rushed out the door and back to the hospital.

I was two minutes late, but my patient was delayed so I had a moment to relax and get my nerves in order. I was usually calm and collected in the operating room but after the exchange with Charlie, I needed to take extra care before opening a young person's chest. I sat in the break room, thinking about Charlie's stubble. I put that same hand up to my face and closed my eyes. Suddenly I was smelling Sandalwood and other spices. It was an outdoorsy smell, mixed with a very sexually arousing male smell. I opened my eyes and could almost picture Charlie, and a great calming sensation fell over me. How is it that I've never noticed his smell before? I closed my eyes one last time, took a deep breath, and was ready to perform my surgery.

I kept my routine of going to JackPot for lunch every Friday and on every Friday, Charlie was there to spend my lunch time with me. The staff had gotten to know my face, and would have my order already prepared by the time I sat down at my table. Charlie would bring out my sandwich and tea, and we would sit there and talk until I was running out of the shop in fear of being late. This went on for almost a month and was a welcome distraction from the hospital that I needed. Charlie and I still haven't exchanged phone numbers. I was wondering when he was going to ask me out, but I didn't press it. I just enjoyed our time and held onto it until the next time I saw him.

Another Friday rolls around and after our normal routine, things changed. We were joking like usual when, out of nowhere, Charlie gets serious. "Em, why did you come back into my life?" It was a very serious question, in need of my most honest answer. I have been waiting on this question for a while, and had the answer already prepared. "I told you that once I got my life in order, I would come looking for you." He smiled at me and I smiled back. "Are you going to run away again, if your life falls out of balance again?"

There it was. This is why he hadn't asked me out again. He's afraid that I will reject him, or run away. I have to provide comfort, but not pity in any way. "I doubt that will happen but if it did, I am in control and won't run away from life again." That seemed to please him because he grabbed my hands and sighed in relief. He brought his hand to my face, bringing along his very tantalizing smell. I leaned into it. "Well, would you let me take you out on a proper date?" I smiled, then gave a nod, so he continued, "How does tonight sound?" I put my hand to his hand that was on my cheek. "That sounds great!" We went back to our regular conversation and enjoyed each other before we had to part. I needed to finish my day at the hospital and then get ready for our date. We finally exchanged phone numbers, and I gave him my address so that he could pick me up.

Charlie arrived promptly at seven p.m. and I was glad, because I had been ready for ten minutes, and I wasn't sure if I could stand to be left alone any longer. So many thoughts swam through my head. I was doubting my clothes and hair, and wondering if it was the best move to enter into a dating relationship with Charlie. I mean, we have been practically dating for a month now. I am just afraid of making it official. What if he finds out that he's not really that into me? I would be so heartbroken, but I would have to move on. Like Harry would say: 'Time moves forward. If you're not moving with it, you risk staying in the past.' I did not want to live in the past, or repeat any of my past offenses. Charlie met me at my door with flowers. I invited him in so that I could put the flowers in some water. He brought me stargazer lilies. I'm not sure how he knew my favorite flower, but it made my heart jump. I felt so in sync with him. It was scary because I have never felt this way with anyone else but, at the same time, I knew this was a great thing and a step in the right direction.

He walked me to his car. He drove a black hybrid SUV. It was freshly washed and manly, which was fitting for Charlie. He opened my door for me, helped me in before walking over to the driver side. When he got in, I asked him where we were going. "Don't worry your pretty little head. I am taking you somewhere I hope you remember." I thought back to where he could possibly be taking me. In the time that we knew each other, we either met at the library, one of our apartments or... what was the name of that place. The name of the little bistro he used to always drag me to. I decided not to ask any more questions. I didn't want him to know that I barely remembered our time together in med school. I just remember the man of my fantasies, and the things that he would do to me in my dreams. We drove in silence for a while. I'm not sure what was going through his mind but for me, I was just anxious about where he was taking me.

We drove for maybe thirty minutes, when we arrived at our destination. The restaurant was small but when I saw the name in lights, the memories started to pour in. I read the sign, "Franchesca's", I can't believe he remembered. Charlie turned to me with his award-winning smile. "So, Em, tell me you remember this place." I looked at him and grabbed his hands. "Of course I remember this place. They used to let us have their whole back room when we came here to study for our labs. I wonder if Aunt Mabel still works here. She was getting up there in age." Charlie gave my hand a little squeeze, "Well, let's go in." Charlie got out of the car and walked around to open my door. He escorted me to the entryway of the restaurant. He opened the door and the smell of garlic bread and pasta sauce blew me away. "Ummm. I wonder if they still serve those cheesy garlic bread knots. They were the best!" We walked up to the hostess desk to wait to be seated. Not too far away, we saw Aunt Mabel setting up one of the tables. I turned and smiled at Charlie, "She's still here!" Charlie gave my shoulders a squeeze and cleared his throat. "Um. excuse me, Miss. We'd like our usual table, if possible."

Aunt Mabel continued setting up the table while she gave us a response. "I'm sorry, you're going to have to be more specific than that." She turned and looked at us. She got a good look at us and then her face lit up. "Oh, my goodness. Look at you two!" She came up to us and gave us each a big hug and then a group hug. "How are you two doing? Are y'all big-time doctors now?"

I let Charlie do all the talking, while I let all the memories flow through me. "Aunt Mabel, so nice to see you. We have both graduated, and are practicing doctors." She waved her hand, "Well, come right in. You are in luck because your usual table is available." We followed her to the back room, where there was a large table sitting in the middle. Aunt Mabel left to get menus and silverware. The room was usually used for large parties or conferences, but it was always our table when we had an important lab coming up and needed nourishment and a place that was open pretty late. Franchesca's was our spot while we were lab partners, and is now our place as a couple, hopefully.

Charlie helped me to my seat before taking his right next to me. I couldn't believe I didn't come back to this place after he and I were no longer in the same classes. Come to think about it, I'm not sure why we weren't even friends. It was all coming back to me. I called him after our first year was up and he ignored my calls, until I just gave up and moved on with my life. I had to find out, because the curiosity would kill me. After we placed our orders, I decided to ask. "Charlie, can I ask you something?" He looked me in my eyes, giving me his full attention. "Em, you can ask anything."

I took a deep breath and sighed. "We had a great time together. Why didn't you ever ask me out? Or why weren't we at least friends? It was like you dropped off the face of the earth." I felt the tears coming, but I told myself to hang it up and don't cry. He hung his head and shook it. "You don't know." It was a statement of fact, not a question. He kept his eyes low and continued, "I received a threatening email from some guy named Greg something, telling me to back off and stop talking to you. I figured he was your boyfriend and I didn't want to interfere, so I ignored your calls until you stopped calling. I didn't mean to hurt you. This guy, whoever he was, sounded really serious and powerful and I didn't want anything to happen to you, or to me, so I cowered."

He finally looked me in my eyes as a tear rolled down. He caught it and said he was sorry if he hurt me. I gave a weak smile, afraid that my face would break and the tears would fall freely. I can't believe it. Greg was controlling my life way before we were together. How could he have done this to me? Now, I have to tell Charlie about Greg on our first date, and hope he doesn't ruin this for me for a second time. "It wasn't your fault. I just underestimated him." Breathing heavily, I continued, "I have to tell you something, and I hope that what I tell you won't change your mind about me. His name was Greg Turner and I recently broke our engagement." I told him everything about Greg. How we met, when we met, how he treated me, him cheating on me when my best friend, and how he cheated on me and my best friend with other women. I even told him about the agreement he and my dad had. I left out the part about the private investigator and Harry. I didn't want him to think I was crazy, too.

"So, Charlie, you see. Greg was the reason I had to get my life together, and why I couldn't bring you into my life a few months ago. I needed time to learn about myself. I needed to learn how to make decisions for myself. I hope this doesn't change how you view me." I gave Charlie a moment to digest the information. He began to speak a few times, but failed to verbalize anything until the fourth try. "So, do you think you're ready for another relationship... so soon after you broke your engagement?" I thought a moment on how best to respond to the question. I was not in love with Greg, and I knew for a long time that he was a cheater. I will always be learning about myself, so I know I have to keep moving so that I will not get left behind.

"A great friend of mine once reminded me that I have to keep moving forward, so that I don't get stuck in the past. I was not in love with Greg because I knew about his infidelity. I'm not even sure I was ever in love with him. I saw my future and I can tell you that I don't think we were meant to be. I am ready to move on, and find that love that was meant for me. If not with you, I know that I am moving in the right direction." He looked at me and smiled, with something that looked like pride. "I have to tell you something, but first you have to answer one question." I gave a puzzling look and said okay. "Do you believe in fate, or in destiny?" Do I believe in fate and destiny? That is a heavy question.

The decisions we make in life cause changes in our future. Indecision, I feel, puts your destiny on hold. Was it fate that Harry walked into my life when he did? So many factors and so many directions the answer to the question can go. So I answered the best way I could, "I'm not sure. I believe all things happen for a reason, so I guess in a way I do believe in destiny." He looked me deep in my eyes. "I think I've been waiting for you my whole life. The moment I met you, I felt a pull toward you. I had a feeling that we would at some point be together. It didn't matter if it was for a day, a year, or forever, it was going to happen and I feel like that time could be right now." He furrowed his eyebrows. "Do you think I'm a complete nut? I mean we just started dating, it's not even official, yet, and I'm talking about forever." I looked him in his eyes and spoke truthfully, "No, and I think our timing is perfect. I am looking forward to every day of happiness you give me, for however long I have it." We sealed the deal with a kiss and when our lips touched, I felt a spark and I knew that he was meant for me.

Epilogue

Five years later...

I sat at the dining room table, looking over at Charlie as he told a story about this man he met and treated at County. He was keeping it PG because our two-year old twin girls, Emily and Charlene, were at the table. My parents were over for dinner, for our traditional Saturday night family meal. I looked over and saw my dad laughing out loud at what Charlie was saying, and my mother trying to laugh into her napkin as she chewed her food. The girls were playing with each other in their highchairs, and I was just sitting there, feeling so thankful. Thankful for my life, thankful for my family and Charlie, and very thankful that Harry showed up when he did. I would never forget Harry. Each day, I give a little thanks to the higher power for bringing him my way.

Charlie and I had what some call a whirlwind romance. He told me he loved me after two months dating officially. We were just wrestling around in the living room of his apartment and when we both stopped to take breaths, he looked at me, brushed a few strands of hair from my face, and said, "Em, I love you." Just like that, and didn't have any expectations in his eyes. I didn't answer. I just pulled him to me and kissed him fiercely. Later that night, while we were in bed falling asleep, I told him I loved him and we made love for the first time.

After three months of dating, I took him with me to my parents' for Sunday brunch. I wasn't sure how my parents were going to react to Charlie. He was not from a family of my status, and had to work his way to pay for school and. to top it off, he worked at County. My mother loved him instantly, because he was charming. She constantly wanted me to bring him by. My father was a little put off, but once he saw how happy Charlie and my relationship made my mother, he started to try to get along with Charlie. I think it was Charlie's charm that won my father over, as well, but he would never say. My father saw the drive, business sense, and love he had for me, so he couldn't deny that Charlie was a much better fit than Greg would ever be. I will never forget what my mother said to me after meeting Charlie. We had excused ourselves to go to the ladies room together, like we were young girls out on a double date or something. When we were far enough away, she took me into an embrace and said, "He's perfect." She was right, Charlie is my perfect match in all ways. We compliment each other and make each other happy, every day. He has never given me any reason to doubt his love, and I am thankful for that. We were engaged six months after that and married the following spring, at my parents' estate.

We enjoyed a little time together, but both knew we wanted to start our family. We sold my townhouse and bought a modest house, closer to my parents. My father wanted to buy a home for us as a wedding gift, but I turned it down because I wanted something to say Charlie and Emma, and nothing else. The house we found was a five-bedroom home, with a large fenced-in backyard, and 2.5 car garage. My father was adamant about purchasing the house so, as a surprise, he paid off my mortgage. I think it was his way of mending our relationship, but it still didn't sit well with me. I made a fuss about it at first, but then Charlie told me that I should let it go because it was apparent that by buying us the house, his weight of guilt was lifted. Of course, Charlie was right. My father was a different person after that, and it just made my life even more complete.

After the house was bought, we wasted no time trying for a baby. It didn't take long for me to get pregnant but, sadly, that pregnancy ended in a first-trimester miscarriage. It was a difficult time for Charlie and I, I thought it would be the event that broke us. I feared the worst. I think I was more worried about what the miscarriage would do to our relation-ship and not necessarily if I would be able to get pregnant again. My Charlie stood by me and showed me what it was to have a real man in my life. He took care of me, and held me close whenever I was crying. He encouraged me to think positively and always let me know that he loved me, even if our life wasn't going to be as we had hoped. I never knew that kind of unconditional love and now that I found it, I didn't care if anything else good came into my life. My parents were also supportive. My mother started coming to the house more often, and being the mother I've always wanted. She confided in me that she suffered two miscarriages before she had me. She said that I was her miracle baby, and her and my father didn't want to try for more kids after I was born, because they felt complete.

When the doctor gave us the go-ahead to start trying again, I was scared of the outcome. We got pregnant on our second month of trying and through the whole first trimester, I ate right, exercised, drank plenty of water, and rested throughout the day. I tried to do everything in my power to make sure that this baby survived. Although I stayed at Handley Medical, I took an extended leave to ensure the safety of my baby.

We made it through the first trimester and then found out that we were having twins. I felt like I was given back the first baby I lost, as well as a sibling to keep them company. We didn't want to know the sex of the babies, but knew the twins were identical, so they were both either boys or girls. Every night, I read them a story and prayed for them to grow big and strong. I was put on bed rest the last month of my pregnancy, and had to undergo a caesarean delivery, but I would not trade the experience for any other. I have two beautiful girls, and a husband that loves me.

To top off all my joy, I will be telling Charlie that he will be a father, once again. I took a home test last week and spoke to my doctor about my blood test this afternoon. I couldn't ask for a better happy ending, and I have Mr. Harold King to thank. I never saw Harry after that first day, but I know if he could see me now, he'd be as proud of me as I am of myself.

Afterword

FROM THE AUTHOR

Not This Time was my gateway into the book publishing world. I have written for most of my life but never imagined that my words would be shared with the world. *Not This Time* was first published in 2018 with the CAMDA company. It was because of Danielle, owner of the CAMDA company, that I found my desire to become an Indie Author and learn the self-publishing process for myself.

I received praise for *Not This Time* but was always approached with the same question: *What is Lyn's deal?* Everyone who has read *Not This Time* hated Lyn, but wanted to know more about her.

Fueled by my readers, I decided to reprint *Not This Time* to make corrections and provide the reader with a short story about Lyn. Without further adieu, I present to you, Redemption: Lyn's story.

Redemption

LYN'S STORY

I draw my knees up so that I can get my legs closer to my body. I rest my chin on top of my knees. My life is over. My mother always told me that having a man to take care of me was more important than any of the bitches I hung out with. I saw how my mom had men falling over her, and giving her whatever she wanted, and when Greg began to do the same for me, I felt like I had found the one. Greg and I just happened. I was not purposely going after my best friend's boyfriend. One thing led to another. One passionate night turned into hundreds of nights, and promises of more to come. It no longer mattered that he was with Emma. I knew that he didn't love her, and the things that she would confide in me about their relationship told me that they wouldn't last. I'm a patient person. I thought if I waited for Greg to break things off, and ensured that Emma was over him, I could slip in and stake my claim.

Emma's last words still haunt me: *I just want to remind you that you said you would never turn into your mother, and here you are.* It's true. I remember crying on Emma's shoulder after our high school graduation. My mother had not shown up to see me walk across the stage. I had to get a ride home with Emma and her parents, because she didn't bother showing up. I was broken. I walked into a dark, quiet home, only to find my mother passed out drunk on the couch. Well, she was barely on the couch. The top half of her body hung awkwardly, floating toward the carpet. Her long beautiful jet-black hair covered her face and when I tried to move her to a comfortable position on the couch, her flowing locks revealed a frightful face, covered in yesterday's makeup. In a lucid moment, my mother revealed that Frankie, her most recent love interest and bank account, had decided to call it quits and try and fix his marriage. Tears flowed freely, and in her alcohol-induced stupor, my mother cried herself back to sleep. I left and went to my thinking place, on the hill behind our house. This was nothing new. My mom would get pushed aside for a newer or younger model and she would drink herself stupid. Then, within 24-hours, she would once again be back out there, getting her claws into her next victim. Emma found me on the hills a few hours later. I had told her enough on previous occasions, that she knew what to expect. On that hill, with my best friend, I vowed never to become my mother. In many ways, I couldn't help taking on some of her characteristics, but I never thought that I would go after an involved man, and hurt my best friend in the same process. Not having Emma in my life feels wrong. If I'm honest with myself, she's the only person that believed in me, now who's going to believe in me?

"I'm sorry. Am I interrupting something?" Her words echo in my mind. The moment she caught Greg and I together continues to replay, and I can't get the image of Emma's expression out of my head. It said that she had already known, and had a bomb to drop, and boy did she drop a bomb. I couldn't prevent the lies from spilling from my mouth. I did not want her, of all people, to see me as less than, and now I am nothing.

I reach for the folder that's sitting on the arm of the chair. I breathe in Emma's scent. It smelled of home and safety. I wipe a scant tear from my eye and try to focus on the envelope. Inside, there is evidence of Greg's infidelities against Emma, and I am amongst the women that defiled their relationship. I open the flap and pull a stack of papers out. The first things I notice are emails between me and Greg. *I am a rotten friend.* At a glance, the memories of writing and responding to these emails adds another dagger to my heart. I violated our friendship by giving her boyfriend the fuel to pull away from her. I throw the papers as far away from me as possible. Images of Greg with countless women cascade across my wood floors. Tears begin to fall and I let out a scream, wishing that the pain in my heart would either cease, or kill me. My cell phone dings and for a moment, my chest swells with the hope that it is Emma. I detach myself from the chair cushion and reach for my phone. It's another text message notification. I have fifteen texts, all from Greg. It baffles me that he thinks that I can go back to him after what has happened with Emma. I open messaging and read the most recent messages. Most are of him begging, but the last one causes me to pause. He is telling me that he has broken it off with the other women and can't get me off his mind. His exact message reads: *The situation was shitty, but it helped me to figure out what I wanted. It's only me and you, now. Please come by.* I sit on the edge of the chair and read the message about twenty more times. Maybe something good has come out of this. My heart feel lighter as I position my fingers to begin typing. I look down at the array of women littering my floor. A dagger twists painfully in my heart, so I put my phone down. This is what I wanted, but the cost, I am not sure it is worth everything that has happened. I tell myself that a walk would help clear my head and make a decision, but deep down, I know that I am going to Max's to see if Greg is there, waiting for me.

I park in the lot behind the buildings and walk toward Max's. The drive over was a blur because my thoughts were solely focused on getting to the bar and reuniting with Greg. There is a twinkle of doubt causing some upset to my stomach. My body buzzes with excitement and trepidation, creating duality between my heart and brain. I feel as if I expect to find Greg there with another woman and my chance with him will disappear, leaving me without a best friend and a boyfriend. Now, I wish I would have stayed home and faced the silence and loneliness, until the feelings passed. But my feet carry me forward and I obey.

I am approaching the large window in front of Max's and the anticipation paralyzes me. My breathing becomes quick and the moment is too much, so I turn around and head in the opposite direction. I stop at the nearest building to catch my breath. "Excuse me, miss. Are you alright?" I look up and find a cheerful older gentleman looking expectantly at me. I take a moment and soak in the concern from his eyes. "I'm fine. I needed a moment to breathe. That's all." I give him a small smile, and he smiles back. I close my eyes and take a few deep breaths. "Looks to me like you've just seen a ghost. That, or you have a lot on your mind." I smile while keeping my eyes closed, "What if it's both?" I laugh, then open my eyes to make sure that I'm not imagining his presence. The old man just looks at me, so I stop laughing. "I recently made some really stupid mistakes and lost the one person who truly loved me. I'm just trying to figure out what to do next." I smile, then frown, lowering my head to my chest.

"It's never too late." I lift my head and look at him with confusion. He grabs my hands and places them between his two deeply wrinkled, yet soft hands, and continues, "It's never too late to start over, or to do what's right. And it's never too late to be happy." He smiles and pats my hands before letting go. For a brief moment, I was lifted through space and time. I felt as if he just gifted me a glimpse into my past and future. Before I could grasp the moment, it was gone. I take a deep look into his eyes and notice for the first time, the wisdom within. "Thank you, Mister--" I look at him questioningly. "Call me Harry." He walks away as he speaks and before I could say another word, I swear I hear him say, "You're welcome, Lyn." I blink and it is as if Harry has disappeared. I look both ways down the street and he is gone. I shake my head, feeling a little off-balance. Max's and Greg are long forgotten as I walk back to my car to head home.

I get back to my house, feeling no closer to a decision than I was before I left. Harry gave me some great advice, but my inner struggle creates more and more confusion. On one hand, Emma hasn't answered any of my calls or texts, so I am sure that our friendship is done. It pains me to think of us never being friends again, but I don't blame her for not taking my calls. I wouldn't take my calls, either. Then, on the other, Greg wants to be with me and only me, and there is no reason not to try a real relationship with him. Although logic tells me that I should not try a real relationship with Greg, my heart sings every time I think about the time we had together. I walk into the living room and sigh when I see the papers strewn across the floor. In my quick escape to locate Greg, I had forgotten about the file. I lazily bend to gather the documents, when a paper with large sums on it catches my eye. I grab it and stand up to read. My mouth falls open when I read that Greg was not, as I thought, a very honest businessman. He had been taking bribes over the years to throw cases, or get clients off, for one reason or another. My eyes scan the paper faster, as I read the details of some of those cases. Like lightning striking, I recall Emma saying that Greg was trying to exploit her and her inheritance. How had I missed this? I try and think back to conversations, or any indication that I felt was dishonest and I find that my memories were all from the aspect of what Greg provided to me. I look around the room, spotting some of those luxury items Greg gifted me over the time we were "dating," and the thought hits me. The money used to buy me gifts was probably not from his paycheck, but rather his payoffs. My anger flares as I pick up my purse and place the paper in it and walk out the door.

I PACE THE FLOOR, wondering if I am making the right decision. I wipe my phone down my pant leg, attempting to get the sweat off the case. I follow this action with wiping my hands down my pant legs, to relieve them of my perspiration. *Just do it,* I tell myself. I press the call button, hoping that the number hasn't changed, and put the phone to my ear, listening to it ring. After the fourth ring, my nervousness turns into sadness. When the voicemail picks up, I'm glad the number hasn't changed, but I am deflated. I had hoped to speak with Emma in person, so that I may invite her out, but since she didn't even answer the phone, I'll leave a message and hope that she could at least forgive me.

Beep.

"Uh, Hi, Em. It's me, Lyn. I really wanted to talk to you in person, but I understand if you never want to see me again. It's been almost two years since our falling out. I really miss you." I laugh because I sound like a sad sap. "I just want to let you know that I understand now. I was my mother, and for that, I'm sorry. I really thought I was in love. I even went looking for the future in the past, but ran into this guy named Harry, instead. He told me it was never too late to do what's right, or to start over. I ignored that advice for a while, but when my heart caught up to my brain, I thought back, and listened. So, I was hoping we could start over. I know, it's silly. Hearing myself say it aloud-- Anyway, I just want you to know that I am truly sorry for breaking our friendship, and your trust. I hope you are well and maybe one day you can forgive me. Well, if I never see you again, I hope that I can at least have your forgiveness. I love--" Beep.

The voicemail service ended the call and I just stared at the screen. The last piece was complete. I sank into my chair, feeling good about everything I have done since that day of indecision. It took some time, but I was finally able to ask for Emma's forgiveness, even if it was via voicemail. I've made peace with my mother, who still believes that I should be out there trying to snag a wealthy man to take care of me. I didn't believe that I could change her mind about men, but hoped she would understand my viewpoints in life. She's up in age and set in her ways, still chasing wealthy men and I love her anyway. I will not live my life as she wants me to. I have decided to, instead, get my degree in Psychology and help those with low self-esteem. It took almost a year for me to realize that I did certain things because I didn't believe I deserved better. After I handled Greg, I took a long look at myself and decided that Harry was right, it is never too late to start over. The little interaction I had with the old man on the street made me realize that I needed someone to talk my problems through with. I found Betty on a flyer while leaving my gynecologist's office. Something about her face made me reach up and grab the flyer, so that no one else would contact her. I went to see my doctor to get tested for every disease under the sun.Who knew what Greg may have exposed me to, and having someone to talk to about the results with will be much better than facing them alone. In my first session, I unloaded the whole Greg situation, leaving little time for getting to know each other. My test results were all negative, and I felt so comfortable sharing my life with this stranger, I still do. Betty is helping me through my issues, and my coursework is helping me solve the mysteries of living a normal and balanced life. Things were finally looking good for me, and I am forgiving myself for what I've done in the past. I am staying in the present.

I hug myself and smile, remembering the progress I've made. There are still some improvements to make, but I will not turn into my mother. I look at my watch and realize that I am close to being late for class. I reluctantly rose from my chair to gather my things. My phone dings just as I grab my backpack from the floor. I glance at the screen. Another message has come through. It's from Emma and it just says, *Harry's a wise man. I forgive you.* I smile and put my phone into my bag and head toward the door. I don't know what this means for the future, but I am forgiven, so the future is bright.

About the Author

Jen Tyes is a Scrum Master at Travelers Insurance and the author of *Not This Time*. When she isn't baking or reading a gripping novel, she can be found watching horror films, hoping for a real scare. After years as a technical writer and subsequently publishing her debut paranormal novel, Jen switched gears to focus on writing speculative and horror fiction. Inspired by her favorite author, Jodi Picoult, she is also an advocate through her blog, www.aim4equanimity.com. Jen lives in Connecticut with her husband and two children. Look for her at www.jentyes.com or follow her on social media.

Also by Jen Tyes

The Light of the Élan Vital

Adam

Beauty Roulette